"Joe Cosentino has a unique and fabulous gift. His writing is flawless, and his use of farce, along with his convoluted plot-lines, will have you guessing until the very last page, which makes his books a joy to read. His books are worth their weight in gold, and if you haven't discovered them yet you are in for a rare treat." — *Divine Magazine*

"a combination of Laurel and Hardy mixed with Hitchcock and *Murder She Wrote*...Loaded with puns and one-liners...Right to the end, you are kept guessing, and the conclusion still has a surprise in store for you." — *Optimumm Book Reviews*

"adventure, mystery, and romance with every page.... Funny, clever, and sweet....I can't find anything not to love about this series....This read had me laughing and falling in love....Nicky and Noah are my favorite gay couple." — *Urban Book Reviews*

"For fans of Joe Cosentino's hilarious mysteries, this is another vintage story with more cheeky asides and sub plots right left and centre....The story is fast paced, funny and sassy. The writing is very witty with lots of tongue-in-cheek humour....Highly recommended." — *Boy Meets Boy Reviews*

"This delightfully sudsy, colorful cast of characters would rival that of any daytime soap opera, and the character exchanges are rife with sass, wit and cagey sarcasm....As the pages turn quickly, the author keeps us hanging until the startling end." — *Edge Media Network*

Drama
Runway

A NICKY AND NOAH MYSTERY

Joe Cosentino

Cover art by Jesús Da Silva
Nicky & Noah Logo by Holly McCabe
Cover and interior design by Fred Wolinsky

★

To Fred for everything,
to the readers who begged
for another Nicky and Noah mystery,
and to everyone who loves to
watch it all hang out on the runway

CAST OF CHARACTERS

**Fashion Ultimate Spring Show
at Treemeadow College:**

Faculty:

Nicky Abbondanza
Professor of Play Directing
Director

Noah Oliver
Associate Professor of Acting
Acting Coach

Martin Anderson
Professor of Theatre
Management
Theatre Department Head
Producer

Tyler Greenway
Associate Professor of
Fashion Design

Ulla Ultimate
Visiting Professor of Fashion
Design
Designer of Fashion Ultimate

Students:

Lila Hekekia
Fashion Design major

Johnny Riley
Fashion Design major

Shane Buff
Fashion Model major

Julio Bonero
Fashion Model major

Cosmo Ferrentino
Fashion Model major

Cory Ultimate
Theatre major
Ulla's son
set designer and model

Hoss Packer
Theatre major
stage manager

Support Staff:

**Taavi Kapule Oliver
Abbondanza**
Nicky and Noah's son
model

Ruben Markinson
Martin's husband
Producer

Shayla Johnson
Theatre Dept Office Assistant

Tia Tedesco
Taavi's girlfriend
seamstress

Miles Jeffrey
Ulla's personal assistant

The Family

**Bonnie (Mom) and
Scott (Dad) Oliver**
Noah's parents

**Valentina (Mama) and
Giacomo (Papa)
Abbondanza**
Nicky's Parents

Bill and Helen Tedesco
Tia's parents

The Law
Detective Jose Manuello

We'll Never Tell

Fay Bene

Macky Mac Mack

Brooke Shills

CHAPTER ONE

The sparkling lights from above illuminated the long stage like stars blanketing an airport runway. Four handsome, young male models, whose bodies were cut like perfect diamonds, strutted down the walkway—lined with flashing lights. Each man was in black leather activewear. One model wore a vest housing tight abs, shorts surrounding a bubble butt, and boots adorning long legs and large feet. Another sported lean muscles under a T-shirt, spiked dog collar, and skintight slacks hosting a palpable bulge. A third spun around in a long flowing coat. The fourth stretched in revealing workout clothes. Each model, with a sensuous glance or a flick of luxurious hair, claimed his section of the runway. The fifth, a young teen, stole the show in black leather jogging shorts and T-shirt as he spun a basketball on his fingertip.

One of the four young men, a bit larger than the rest, slipped a candy bar from his black leather waist pouch. After stealing a bite, he accidentally dropped the wrapping onto the stage floor. The moment his leather heel slid over it, the model took to the air, landing bottom-up at the edge of the runway—mooning the audience. The music for the opening song played: a rock version of "You're Never Fully Dressed Without a Smile."

"Stop!" It's me again, Nicky Abbondanza, PhD—standing for pretty hot daddy—now that I'm forty-two years old, accent on the old. Actually, my students tell me I'm "well preserved for my age." I'm tall, with dark hair, a

Roman nose, emerald eyes, and a cleft chin my hubby loves to tickle with his tongue. Thankfully my body hasn't dropped yet thanks to the gym on campus, which keeps my muscles pumped and my stamina pooped. Also, I'm called "larger than life." It isn't a comment on my witty personality. To the delight of my husband, horror of my tailor, and envy of my gay friends, I have a nearly-foot-long penis when aroused — which happens nowadays as frequently as a student not texting during one of my lectures.

Why is Treemeadow College's Professor of Play Directing rehearsing a fashion runway show? The answer is Ultimate, that's Ulla Ultimate of Fashions Ultimate. Ulla, having conquered the fashion world in Europe and the US, wanted to be a visiting college professor. As the expression goes, "The other man's grass always gives you a better high." Seeking a safe place to try out her controversial new spring line and wanting to be near her Theatre major son, Ulla contacted our college president. He contacted the dean who contacted the head of the Fashion Department who contacted my best friend and head of the Theatre Department, Martin Anderson, who contacted yours truly. After Ulla was hired as a visiting professor, she was offered the fashion show scheduled for spring break. Martin asked me to add some theatrical flair to Ulla's runway. Faster than a priest lassoing an altar boy with rosary beads, I needed to cancel my group's spring break gay cruise to Iraq. This upset my husband, Associate Professor of Acting Noah Oliver, whose thirty-fifth birthday we just celebrated. (*Okay, I'm a cougar.*) Our thirteen-year-old adopted son, Taavi Oliver Abbondanza Kapule, and Martin's husband of an age, Ruben Markinson, also gave me shoulders colder than Uranus. *No pun intended.* That is, until I asked Noah to be the fashion models' acting coach, Ruben to co-produce the runway show with Martin, and Taavi to be a junior model. I, of course, would direct the production to give it the Abbondanza theatrical flair—or curse (*more on that later*).

Unfortunately, my husband, son, and I don't have the gay fashion gene. We each wear a dress shirt, dress slacks, and blazer on a daily basis. However, we definitely have the ham gene. Our little troupe has put on plays, musicals, a murder mystery dinner theatre piece, a luau show, a ballet, and even a couple of movies. So, I assumed a runway show would be easier to piece together than a president's Russian money laundering trail. What could possibly go wrong? *Everything.*

"Cosmo, are you all right?" I asked the junior modeling major as I stared at his butt from my front row center seat.

Average weight, meaning obese in the modeling world, Cosmo Capra popped a button on his leather midriff shirt as he scrambled to his leather soles. "I'm fine, Professor."

"Yeah, Cosmo's phat, Professor." Senior modeling major Shane Buff fluffed his bleached blond hair and batted his contact-lens blue eyes.

"Screw you, Shane!"

The rail thin model aimed his sculpted body at Cosmo. "No thanks. I'm not a chubby chaser."

Senior modeling major Julio Bonero stood at Shane's other shoulder, his onyx eyes focused on Shane. "Big deal. Cosmo is grossly fat. Lay off him."

"Like I laid off you, Julio?" Shane placed a thin hand on his narrow hip.

Julio's tiny abs contorted between his black leather vest. "Don't play with me, Shane."

"That's not what you said last week, dude." Shane giggled.

Velvety black hair covered Cosmo's dark eyes as he reached into the pocket of his waist pouch and pulled out a wrapped cupcake.

After he swallowed it in two bites, I said, "Can

everyone please get back into your starting places for the opening number." Then I called out over their boots banging on the stage floor, "Sing out, and remember Noah's choreography."

"Let your eyes make love to the audience." Noah, sitting next to me, continued to instruct the student models. "Use emotional recall to remember a time when you were empowered, sexy, in control."

Shane smirked. "I felt that way when I broke up with Julio — and he begged me not to leave him."

Julio's fists clenched, and tiny biceps appeared under his black leather T-shirt. "Don't push me too far, Shane."

"Or?"

"Or I'll tell daddy butch Buff his favorite son is a fashion major, not a business major."

Shane met Julio chiseled face to chiseled face, like two gay cowboys in a Hollywood movie destined for an Oscar nomination. "You do that, Julio, and it'll be the last time you drag your scrawny ass down this runway — or any runway."

"Fine with me. I'm only modeling to get into acting."

Shane chuckled. "Good luck with that."

Julio glared at him. "You'll be sorry when I have my own TV show — with no guest spot for *you*."

I cleared my throat. "Please go back to your opening positions offstage, or I'll have to cut some of you from the opening number!"

The models disappeared backstage faster than a family values politician cheating on his third wife. I asked, "Hoss, are the lights ready to go again?"

Hoss Packer, junior theatre major, sat in a lighting booth toward the rear of the audience section with his huge muscles nearly bursting out of a cherry T-shirt and jeans. "Ready, Professor." His dark skin, hair, and eyes nearly disappeared as the first lighting cue dimmed the theatre.

"Cory, how is the set holding up?" Hearing no reply, I

shot Noah a worried glance, and he squeezed my hand. Let me explain. All nine of our past productions had the same minor problem—five murders committed in each. While nobody enjoys a good murder mystery investigation more than yours truly, I was hoping this show would break the cycle.

"Cory?"

Cory Ultimate, sophomore theatre major, appeared onstage in his black leather workout outfit. His mussed chestnut hair, baby face, and hot body gave him a roguish charm. Zipping his bulbous fly, he said, "I was in the dressing room helping Shane take his clothes off." Adorable dimples immerged. "I mean…put his clothes on—again."

I sighed. "Is the set holding up all right?"

Cory gazed in admiration at his creation of a dungeon backdrop on stage. "I think it's totally hot." He winked at the lighting booth. "Like Hoss."

Hoss groaned.

I changed the subject. "Thanks for doing double duty (*try saying that three times fast with dentures*) as our set designer and model, Cory."

He licked his full lips like a cat at a sushi bar. "I'm happy to be in the action, Professor."

"Let's take the opening number again from the top."

Cory disappeared backstage. The models reentered and got through the song. All went well—except for the lights going out at the models' entrance, Shane entering late with a used condom dragging from one heel, Cosmo smiling with pieces of brownie caught between his teeth, Julio tripping Shane during a dance break, and the dungeon set falling down at the models' exit.

I asked myself why I never became a ditch digger. "Thank you, everyone. Let's call it a night. I'll see you all back tomorrow at ten a.m."

As the models exited the runway for the dressing room

backstage, my handsome husband rested a warm arm around my shoulder. His golden blond hair smelled of strawberry shampoo. "The show will come together by opening, Nicky."

"So will the acid in my esophagus."

"At least everyone is safe."

I sniggered. "Have we come to the point of being thankful nobody in our show has been murdered?"

"Small favors."

I gazed into his true-blue eyes. "How come I'm lucky enough to always have you by my side?"

"Because I'm absolutely nuts about you." He kissed my chin. "And because we're carrying on the Treemeadow tradition."

I'll explain for you newbies and repeat for you regulars having a senior moment. Harold Tree and Jacob Meadow were a gay couple who founded our Treemeadow College in picturesque Treemeadow, Vermont—a place where white church steeples reaching for the clear blue sky are seen as frequently as cozy bookstores, cozy cafes, and just about cozy anything.

"And *we're* part of the Treemeadow tradition too." My best friend and department head, Martin Anderson, small, bald, and birdlike, sat behind me. He wore his usual sweater vest and bowtie, chartreuse today.

"Yes, Martin is as old as the bronze statues of the founders at the entrance of the college." Martin's husband, Ruben Markinson, sat next to him wearing a chartreuse leisure suit that fit his regal demeanor.

Undaunted, Martin waved a thin finger at his husband. "It is quite fitting that we produce a fashion show. *I* was a print model in my youth."

Ruben ran a hand through his gray hair. "That's amazing."

"My youth as a male model?"

"That, and your ability to remember so far back."

Martin stared off into the distance as if signaling a flashback scene in a movie. "I remember it well, including modeling for some very prestigious magazine ads."

"Did you play a terminally ill patient for a hospital ad, or a fruit in an underwear ad?"

Martin sniffed at his husband. "I sold many different products."

"For incontinence?"

"For fashion!" Martin rested his hands under a wrinkled neck. "Had I been taller, I could have been a runway model."

"I can see that."

Martin kissed his spouse's cheek. "Thank you, Ruben."

"I can see you walking onstage and everyone in the audience running away."

As Martin and Ruben continued their war of the roses behind us, our son appeared in front of us. Out of his black leather jogging outfit, and back in his dress shirt, dress slacks, and blazer, Taavi played coy. "Was I okay up there, Pop?"

I rose and kissed his olive-colored cheek. "You were terrific, and you know it."

Noah joined me, beaming with pride. "You were the only model who executed the choreography perfectly, and you always had facial animation."

Taavi looked happier than a dentist the day after Halloween. "Thanks, Dad."

Noah mussed our son's dark hair. "You've had quite a career for a thirteen-year-old."

"And this show is the most special." Taavi offered us a lovesick smile. "Tia is interested in fashion design and modeling. She's helping out in the sewing room."

I replied, "With so many clothing repairs and alterations needed, we can use the help."

"Taavi!"

Noah, Martin, Ruben, and I stood reverently as Ulla

Ultimate made her way from the center of the house (*meaning the seating area*). Thanks to an obvious facelift and cheekbone implants at only forty-one years old, she appeared like a chipmunk overdosing on acorns. Rail thin, Ulla's white face, black eye makeup and nail polish, platinum straight wig, and black leather midriff corset and skirt caused her to appear as a character in an old horror movie. She patted Taavi's head as if a puppy's. "I was watching you. You're a good boy. And more importantly, a good model. You instinctively understand that every move on the runway must be magic, as you weave each piece of fabric into fantasia."

I explained, "Our son has been in show business since we adopted him in Hawaii when he was seven years old."

Ulla's violet eyes glistened. "You've both brought him up well."

Noah and I shared a hug. Taavi offered her the hang loose sign.

"I wish I could say the same about *my* son." Ulla gazed over to the stage, where Cory Ultimate flirted with Julio Bonero. "I designed and sewed during Cory's childhood. Now *he* appears to be doing the designing and sowing—of his wild oats. I have been away in Europe. I came back hoping he'd be over this by now. Clearly, I hoped in vain."

Cory batted his long eyelashes at Julio. "So, you want to be an actor?"

"More than anything," Julio replied.

"Lots of actors started out as models."

Julio nodded. "And modeling helps me feel comfortable performing in front of people."

"It's really important to feel comfortable around people. Like right now, I feel really comfortable around you." Cory placed his hands on Julio's bottom. "Do you feel comfortable with me?"

Julio moved Cory's hands off him. "I do now."

"That's too bad. I felt more comfortable before." Cory

tented his fingers. "And when I feel comfortable, I'm more apt to talk to some of my mother's friends in the television industry and recommend a new actor to them."

Julio glowed like a meteor crashing into a shooting star. "Would you do that for *me*?"

"Only if I feel comfortable with you. *Very* comfortable."

Ulla called out, "Cory, may I speak with you a moment?"

He strutted down the runway and came down the stairs, facing his mother.

Ulla said like a general addressing a private, "Your behavior with Julio is out of line. Stop it."

"But don't you have friends in the television business, Mother?"

"Yes, but you have no right to dangle that in front of the other models."

Cory smirked. "Actually, I've been dangling something else in front of them."

She scowled. "Grow up, Cory. Haven't you tired by now of saying and doing things to try to shock and repulse me?"

He blinked back tears. "I'm sorry I repulse you, Mother."

Ulla softened. "Cory, the set you designed for my show is lovely. And you look fine in your outfits."

He seemed surprised. "You noticed?"

"I notice everything."

"Except your son."

Ouch!

Ulla's pale face reddened. "Do you really need to go into your theatrics here and now in front of others?"

Always ready for good gossip, Martin cried out, "Please do. Don't mind us."

Ruben pulled his husband down into their seats.

Cory unleashed a dazzling smile at us. "Our esteemed director, acting coach, and producers should hear all about how the famous Ulla Ultimate devoted her life to the world of fashion, while her son learned to fend for himself."

She grasped his arm. "Come back to my hotel suite and we can talk."

"I'm staying at the dorm." He tapped his index fingers together. "However, in whose room, I can't say."

"May I escort you to the hotel, Ulla?" A tall, thin, young man with broad shoulders filling an expensive-looking three-piece gray suit appeared next to Ulla.

Cory folded his arms over his wide chest, and his biceps expanded like grapefruits. "Who's he?"

Ulla pointed as if Exhibit A. "This is Miles Jeffrey, my personal assistant."

"What happened to Pierre?" Cory asked.

"He had family obligations in Paris and resigned."

Cory sneered at his mother. "Imagine that, Mother, family obligations. Actually taking care of your children instead of burying yourself in your work."

Miles' long, pointy nose aimed in Cory's direction. "I think you've said enough."

"Oh, you do, do you?"

Try saying that three times fast with a new hairdo.

"Your mother's had a long day." Miles met Cory's glare. "She needs a break. Can you give her one?"

In an effort to cut the thick air, we each introduced ourselves to Miles. "I'm Nicky Abbondanza, the director."

"Noah Oliver, the acting coach, and Nicky's husband."

"Taavi Oliver Abbondanza Kapule, teen model." He posed like a superhero with his fists on his hips. "And the most talented member of the family."

As we all shook Miles' large hand, Martin leaned forward and offered his hand like a queen (*pun intended*). "We're Martin and Ruben, producers and husbands. But don't mind us. Continue the drama, everyone."

Ulla reclaimed her audience. "In the short time Miles has worked for me thus far, he has impressed me a great deal."

"Unlike your son, who sickens you?" Cory pouted.

Ulla seemed more determined than a conservative politician wiping out a scientific report. "Cory, Miles is doing so well that in addition to his taking care of my business needs, I've given him a...personal task."

Martin shot up from his chair faster than the deficit rising after the election of a Republican president. "Did you say a 'personal' task?"

"Down, boy." Ruben stood next to his husband.

Ulla explained, "Cory, I certainly understand that young people need to...play the field. I did some of that myself when I was in college. But those who play into overtime generally find themselves losing the game."

Taavi scratched his dark hair. "I don't understand."

"You don't need to." Martin waved Ulla on, salivating at the prospect of getting some new gossip. "We're listening."

"You think I don't care about you? You're wrong. I've been quite concerned about your antics." Ulla continued as if a judge reaching a verdict. "Cory, you've sown enough wild oats to make oatmeal to feed a third world nation. I thought long and hard about what to do about it. Here is my decision. I've given Miles the task of finding you a husband. Hopefully someone as responsible as Noah."

I pulled Noah into me and asked Miles, "How will you accomplish your task?"

"Ulla has told me a great deal about Cory. I also plan to interview him myself." Miles' long finger moved charts around a handheld computer tablet. "I'm seeking the perfect ying to Cory's yang."

Ruben glanced over at Cory's bulging crotch. "He has quite a yang."

Martin pushed his shoulder. "Which *you'll* never see."

Ulla continued. "Miles will interview all the single, young, gay men here at Treemeadow during spring break, until he finds the perfect mate for my son."

"And if he doesn't?" Martin licked his full red lips.

Ulla unveiled a plastic white smile. "He will."

Cory glared at his mother. "We're not Moonies. You can't *arrange* a marriage for me!"

"No, but I can cut off every cent that goes to you now and after I'm dead, if you don't agree to date whomever Miles selects for you."

Cory's face hardened. "Are you sure you want to do that, Mother?"

"Positive."

Norman Bates anyone?

Cory stumbled backward a few steps. After regrouping, he approached Miles. "You're not hooking me up with some dweeb."

Miles offered a thin smile. "I plan to follow your mother's orders and find the right man for you."

"All right." Cory played along. "I like hot, dangerous guys with a wild streak." Cory's dimples looked like craters. "You want to know about me? Here's my motto. I think of men like pancakes. You flip the first one over to warm your griddle and prepare you for the whole stack."

That gives new meaning to 'a hot man.'

Miles came pointy nose to wide nose with him. "Get some rest, little boy. I'm starting my interviews tomorrow. Your mom wants you to settle down. So settle down."

"You can't tell me what to do."

"We'll see about that. I think you've met your match, Cory. Goodnight, gentlemen." Miles led Ulla through the side door into the lobby and out of the theatre.

Cory made his way over to Hoss who was coming out (*no pun intended*) of the lighting booth. He licked his lips at the sight of the tall, muscular theatre major. "Just what I'm in the mood for. A hunk of delectable dark chocolate. Placing his arms around Hoss's thick neck, Cory pressed his pelvis against the stage manager's. "Share your candy with me, Hoss?"

After moving Cory's arms back to his own side, Hoss said, "I'm interested in your lighting designs, not your designs on me." He headed to the door. "Goodnight, Professors."

Cory stomped back up the stairs, onto the runway, and disappeared backstage.

"Well that was fun." Martin clasped his arm through Ruben's. "Let's go home and dish the dish. Goodnight, Nicky and Noah."

After Martin and Ruben were gone, I kissed my husband and son, and asked Noah to drive Taavi home. Then standing alone in the darkened theatre, I envisioned the runway show as it should be, hoping we could get there by week's end. Theatres always held a mystical aura for me. There is nowhere I'd rather be than alone in a darkened theatre. It's my haven, my church, my place of wonder and magic.

I stood before the runway and lifted my head toward the lighting equipment and then forward at the resurrected dungeon set framed by scarlet curtains. Satisfied with my theatre fix, I headed toward the back door and left. It was a beautiful spring day just before sunset. Palettes of jasmine, peach, and vermillion painted the sky, which served as a backdrop for the Kelly mountains and azure lake in the distance. Realizing I left my notepad and pen in the theatre and wanting to go over my notes for the models and tech crew, I headed back to the Fashion Department building and into the theatre. As I opened the back door, I noticed the silhouette of a young woman onstage. Flowing blonde hair caressed her beautiful face, and an elegant white gown covered her soft body. I hid in the darkness as she glided down the runway more graceful than a Giselle. I couldn't take my eyes off the mesmerizing model as she spun, dipped, glided, and finally disappeared.

I left the theatre again. As I walked across campus, past

the Edwardian white stone buildings surrounded by the low white stone wall, I couldn't get my mind off the phantom model. Was she an apparition? A figment of my exhausted imagination? If not, who was she? All of our models in the spring-break show were male. She plagued my thoughts as I walked between the bronze statues of our college's founders, into the parking lot, and drove home.

The sight of our, rather the college's, honey-colored Victorian home always brought a smile to my face, and an ache to my calves as I mounted the steps to the wraparound porch. I entered the house to Noah and Taavi waiting for me in our dining room, complete with flowered wallpaper and oak wainscoting—the dining room, not Noah and Taavi. After a delicious dinner of cedar plank wild salmon, shitake mushrooms, lemon and garlic brown rice, and gingered carrots and string beans in a sweet miso reduction, I was glad not to be a starving model.

After dinner, we loaded the dishwasher—a happy addition to our Victorian home—and mounted the flared oak staircase. Next, I sat in my cozy study at the cozy roll-top desk opposite the cozy brick fireplace adjacent to the cozy window seat. After going over my notes from the rehearsal, I gazed out the window and noticed the sky had turned the mountains and lake into a cobalt shadow. I wondered if that was a foreshadowing of things to come.

I met up with Noah in Taavi's bedroom down the hall. We each sat on opposite sides of Taavi's sleigh bed. I took the cell phone out of our son's still-texting hand and placed it on the night table. Noah pulled the sheet over Taavi, who was dressed in our usual sleepwear: boxers and a T-shirt. Noah said, "You really like Tia, huh?"

Taavi nodded, and thick dark hair covered his forehead. "She's so cool."

I asked, "Would you like us to invite Tia's parents and Tia over to dinner some night?"

He looked more excited than a high schooler during a

bomb scare. "That would be really cool!"

My son the poet.

Noah stroked the hair away from Taavi's eyes. "What do you like about Tia?"

Taavi leaned up on one elbow. "We're in the same class at school." He smirked. "When we're not off for spring break. And we both like the same thing."

"Skyping endlessly?" I asked.

"Texting to early arthritis?" Noah added.

"Planning our futures."

Noah tucked the sheet under his chin. "What are your plans?"

Taavi's dark eyes lit up like marbles under a lamp. "I'm going to be an actor, director, and crime solver—like you two guys."

Like fathers, like son.

"And Tia?" Noah asked.

"Tia likes theatre, especially fashion. She wants to be a costume designer."

I was impressed Taavi gave Tia's future some consideration too.

He grinned. "So, she can design the costumes for my plays, movies, ballets, and runway shows."

He's one of the family.

Noah and I each kissed a cheek and wished Taavi goodnight. When we got to the door, I shut the light.

"Pop?"

"What is it?"

"Who do you think will be murdered first?"

I did a doubletake. "Nobody is going to be murdered."

Taavi cocked his head. "You're directing the show, Pop. You know what always happens."

Noah placed a reassuring hand on my shoulder. "Hopefully nobody will get hurt, and the tenth show will be the charm."

From your mouth to the mystery gods' ears.

We wished Taavi pleasant dreams—without murders

in them. Then I shut the door, and Noah and I made our way down the hall into our bedroom.

After we peeled off our clothes, we met at the center of our large fourposter with the stars waving at us from the window. I wrapped my arms around Noah and I was home. "It seems like our son is smitten."

Noah rested his golden locks on my chest and I smelled strawberries. "Just like his father."

"And his other father."

We shared a soft kiss that reached down to my toes. I lowered Noah onto his back and lay on top of him, our erections signaling what was ahead. He ran his fingers through my hair and kissed the cleft in my chin. "You are my world."

"The world is only you and me."

My tongue explored the familiar sweetness of his smooth hair, thick earlobes, and soft cheeks. When our lips met, our dueling tongues lavished in their warm caverns. After Noah massaged my back muscles and kneaded my pecs and abs, I worked my way down his velvety neck to caress his silky chest. When my lips tugged on his hard nipples, Noah let out a cry signaling he wanted more. I was happy to oblige. Reaching his golden bush, I kissed every inch of his long, thin, curved manhood, finally devouring the prize as Noah wiggled and writhed in ecstasy. "I'm going to —"

I pulled away. "No you're not—yet!" Coming to my knees, I dangled my prize over Noah's face. Faster than a factory worker leaving at the closing whistle, Noah opened his mouth wide and greedily devoured my mushroom head, taking more and more of me until he gagged in delight. After sliding out, I lifted Noah's legs into the air and entered the man of my heart slowly but firmly.

He responded by holding onto my thigh muscles as if they were life rafts in a storm. "I want every inch of you. Only you."

"Only me." Happily complying, I pushed in deeper and deeper. With each thrust, Noah whimpered in delight, lifting his pelvis toward me, begging for more. When my head, both of them, were ready to explode, I reached out for Noah. My love exploded inside of him as he reciprocated in my hand. After we collapsed onto each other, I kissed his shoulder and he licked my ear. "You're the reason my heart beats."

He sighed happily. "My heart beats only for you."

After we kissed, washed up in our bathroom, and cuddled back in bed, I sat up with my back against the headboard. "I hope Taavi finds the same love we've found."

"And that it doesn't take him as long to find it as it took us." Noah rested his head on my shoulder. "Do you think Tia's the one?"

"They're thirteen years old."

"Romeo and Juliet were teenagers."

"They didn't turn out so well."

Noah sat up cross-legged. "I guess it could be puppy love."

I shrugged. "They seem to have a lot in common, and they both enjoy the same thing—Taavi."

"It's not easy being an actor's spouse."

"Tell me about it."

He playfully slapped my arm. "It's nice of Tia to help out with the fashion show."

"Especially nice for Taavi." I snickered. "I wonder how she sews and texts at the same time."

"Do you want to call her parents to invite them all over, or should I?"

"You can. When we met them at the last show, the mother seemed to have her eye on you." I kissed his cheek. "Who can blame her?"

"You have a vivid imagination, which I love." He returned the kiss. "I'll call Mrs. Tedesco." Then staring out the window at the silver stars glowing in the charcoal sky, Noah seemed miles away. "I wonder if Taavi's right."

"About what?"

"Production number ten being like the other nine. Nicky, we may have nine lives, but I doubt we have ten."

I placed my arm around him. "Nobody's been murdered in this show."

"Yet."

I rested my head back. "But I *have* witnessed some…conflict among the players."

He grinned. "You think?"

As a play director and amateur sleuth, the psychology behind a character's actions has always intrigued me. "Did you notice Shane Buff and Julio Bonero are exes."

"To Julio's chagrin." Noah rubbed his adorable chin. "Do you think Julio will spill the beans to Shane's father about Shane being a fashion major rather than a business major?"

"Not if Shane has anything to say about it." I sighed. "Ah, the life of a student male model."

"The life indeed. I'm sure you caught our student set designer slash model trying to sneak some sugar with Julio after rehearsal."

"We were meant to catch that."

"What do you mean?"

"It was as contagious and obvious as the flu." I pressed my knees against my chest. "Cory Ultimate put on that little charade with Julio to anger his mother. He's acting out to get her attention."

"Why would the great Ulla Ultimate care that her son wants to get it on with another college student?"

"Ulla's obviously as controlling a mother as she is a fashion designer. Sometimes it's easier to control those we love than to listen to them and respect their own path in life."

Noah played footsies with me. "Cory's path seems to

be a winding one."

"And his mother apparently wants him to walk straight—to the altar." I laughed. "Can you believe Ulla actually gave her personal assistant the task of interviewing candidates to marry her son?"

"Sure. My mother threatened that once."

"She did?"

Noah nodded. "Just before I met you."

I chuckled. "Your dad would have asked me what movies I like. And your mom would have wanted to know if her friend Judy in Wisconsin approved of me."

"Your papa would have grilled me on my favorite Italian pastry. And your mama would have asked if I know 'Carmine the Mooch with the golden cannoli.'"

We shared a laugh.

I sobered up. "We're lucky to have such supportive parents—who live far away from Vermont, in Wisconsin and Kansas."

Always giving everyone the benefit of the doubt, my sweet-hearted husband said, "I think Ulla cares about her son, but she can't separate love from dominance."

"Maybe Cory needs someone to dominate him."

"Don't we all." Noah giggled.

I pinched his pec. "Do you think we'll be ready for the show?"

"We always are." He kissed my nose. "Thanks to the magic of show business."

"If Cosmo Capra doesn't stop eating, the sewing staff will need to reinforce all of his outfits."

"Poor guy. I wonder why he eats so much. There must be something bothering him."

"Yeah, Shane and Julio mocking him for putting food into his mouth."

Always concerned for others, Noah's handsome face saddened. "Why do models have to be so thin?" He winked at me. "I like a man with some meat on his bones."

"Then you must like our student stage manager. Hoss Packer is built bigger than an actor on daytime television during sweeps week."

"Cory Ultimate sure seemed to notice."

"Cory was more stimulated than a closet gay man watching a bodybuilding contest from the front row with binoculars and a raincoat."

We both burst out laughing.

"Nicky, we sound like Martin and Ruben."

"Minus the arguing."

He used Ruben's crisp delivery. "Are you still able to argue at your age?"

We guffawed again and slid down onto our white satin sheets. The moment our heads rested on our hypoallergenic pillows, I remembered. "I think I saw a ghost tonight."

Noah did a doubletake.

"When I was alone in the fashion department theatre. It was dark. A beautiful young woman all in white nearly floated down the runway." I sighed. "I was tired. Maybe it was a daydream."

"Fantasies of a woman? How unlike you." He kissed one of my long sideburns. "Should I be worried?"

"Hardly." I spooned him in my arms. "I probably imagined it." *Or maybe it was a foretelling of what's to come.* As Noah snored softly, I thought about our cast and crew for the runway show. Like Taavi, I wondered which one of them would be murdered first.

CHAPTER TWO

I woke the next morning shaken from flashbacks of celestial dreams about the model in white. After showering and drying off, I stood naked before the Victorian floor-length mirror in our bathroom and applied my new skin cream.

Already dressed, Noah entered behind me (*no pun intended*) with a smirk on his adorable face. "Skin cream? Planning on becoming a model?"

"I read an online gay magazine. There was an article about anti-aging techniques. Actually, *every* article was about anti-aging techniques."

He peered around my shoulder to run a comb through his long golden locks. "You smell good. What's in that stuff?"

I searched for the ingredients list on the jar. After reading a diatribe of harmful ingredients not in the lotion, I finally found the list. "Aloe vera, calendula, echinacea, green tea, lavender, peach, cherry, cinnamon, vanilla, and other natural ingredients."

"It sounds good enough to eat." Noah took the jar from my hand and rested it on the side of our clawfoot tub. "But, Nicky, I'll always love you, no matter how old, wrinkled, and cranky you become."

I slapped his backside. "The lotion feels nice on my skin."

His aqua eyes twinkled like sunshine reflecting on a lake. "As nice as me?"

"Almost as nice as you."

"Would you like some help applying the lotion?"

"Only on my private parts."

He giggled. "Then I'm your man."

Later, after dressing, we hurried downstairs to the kitchen nook and ate our breakfast (eight-grain vanilla cream French toast with strawberries and pecans). Since Noah is allergic to nuts (but clearly not mine when they're covered in skin lotion), I ate his pecans. Taavi texted feverishly to Tia as we finished breakfast. Once I swallowed my stack of vitamins with a peach mango smoothie chaser, we cleaned up the kitchen and headed out the front door.

Noah drove his sportscar faster than someone mentally ill purchasing a machine gun. We parked and walked through the gates celebrating our college's gay founders. Then we made our way along the cobblestone walkway with the low white stone fence shielding us from the glimmering lake and stoic mountains in the distance. The smells of early-budding spring flowers filled our nostrils as we passed various academic buildings, including the theatre building, and finally the fashion building.

We entered through the door behind the building and came to what the fashion students affectionately called "the sweatshop." Taavi rushed over to Tia, sitting at a machine on the far side of the shop. Noah said hello to Tia and then walked over to the dressing room, no doubt to give the models much needed acting notes.

I approached freshman fashion major Johnny Riley who sat behind a sewing machine near the door. His periwinkle T-shirt and jeans hung off him like big and tall clothes on a child mannequin. As he repaired a black leather jacket, his mop of bright red hair covered shamrock green eyes and more freckles than voting machine outages in big cities during elections. With bandages on most of his fingers, the eighteen-year-old seemed more frazzled than a childless employee on Take Your Child to Work Day. I asked, "Is everything all right, Johnny?"

"Owww!" He sucked the blood off an already bandaged thumb. "I'm fine, Professor. Yikes!"

"You don't seem fine."

He searched for a bandage in the nearly empty first-aid kit on his sewing table. "I can't seem to get the hang of working with leather. Threading the needle punctured a few of my fingers. Running the sewing machine stabbed the rest of them. But I should be okay. I took an iron pill."

I sat at the edge of a work table facing him and noticed the bandage on Johnny's arm. "How did *that* happen?"

"A mannequin fell on me when I tried to dress it. The swelling and purple marks should go away soon." Finished with the jacket, the thin young man rose to hang it with other outfits on a clothing rack—which fell on top of him.

"Ow!" He propped up the rack and then limped back to his sewing table.

"Why are you limping?"

"When I was sweeping up last night, the broom knocked into my leg and I fell on a spiked dog collar."

"Which is why your cheeks are scratched?"

"That's from falling into the dye bin when I was treating fabric. It wasn't too bad. My cheeks only bled for about an hour." He sighed. "But there's still lots to do."

"Johnny, relax, the clothes for the show will be fine."

"So will the show." Hoss Packer entered from outside with his muscles rippling out of a tangerine T-shirt and jeans.

I said, "My stage manager, just who I want to see. Last night I emailed you a list of notes for the lighting and sound cues."

Hoss lifted the laptop in his hand, and his bicep looked like a chocolate mountain. "I have them all, Professor." He unleashed a warm smile. "Rehearsal will go better today."

It couldn't go any worse.

Hoss leaned against Johnny's sewing table, and his pecs nearly exploded out of his T-shirt. "How are the alterations coming, Johnny? We don't want any more models unintentional mooning the audience."

Johnny's face turned beet red.

Or is it more blood stains?

"Excuse me." The freshman raced out of the room.

Hoss's handsome face registered concern. "Was it something I said?"

I patted his shoulder, which felt like steel. "We're all a bit on edge with the show coming up."

"I know *I'm* on edge." Shane Buff sauntered over from the adjacent dressing room. He wrapped his arms around Hoss's waist. "Care to calm me down, Hoss?"

Julio Bonero appeared in Shane's shadow. "You're making a fool of yourself, Shane."

Shane guffawed. "Like you made a fool of yourself begging me not to dump you?"

Julio rested a hand on Hoss's broad back. "A terrific guy like Hoss wouldn't want anything to do with you, Shane. I'm guessing he's interested in someone with a future in television." He winked at Hoss. "Someone like me."

"Do you think Hoss would want *you*, Julio?" Shane yanked at Hoss's thick forearm. "*I'm* more Hoss's type." He added in Hoss's ear. "You're too hot for my cold leftovers."

Getting free, Hoss said, "I'm interested in *both* you guys."

Johnny came out of the bathroom, gasped, and ran back inside.

"I'd consider a threesome with Julio, Hoss." Shane giggled. "If *you* can be in the middle for a dark meat sandwich." He added, "You know what's so cool about being a male model? Males."

Julio groaned. "Hoss is A-list, and you're D-list, Shane."

"Coming from a Z-lister," Julio's ex replied.

Julio glared at Shane. "Wouldn't daddy Buff just love to hear about his D-list son, the fashion major, and his new crush, the black theatre major? Guess who's coming to dinner, Papa?"

"You vicious queen!"

Hoss raised his large hands to stop Shane from attacking Julio. "What I meant was that I'm interested in both of you as models in the show. Nothing more."

Four shoulders slumped.

I piped up. "Shane, Julio, why don't you get into your outfits for rehearsal?"

Shane winked at Hoss. "I'll be in the dressing room — if you want to undress me."

Julio sighed. "Can't you see the guy isn't into you, Shane?"

"Can't you see *I'm* not into *you*, Julio?"

Julio looked like a little boy who lost his favorite toy. "You were...once."

"And once was enough."

Julio tugged at Shane's arm. "Are you saying that because of Cory Ultimate?"

"What are you talking about, dude?"

"I saw Cory coming out of your dorm room this morning."

"Cory came *inside* my dorm room last night." Shane laughed at his own joke. "No worries, Julio. Even if my bed were empty, I wouldn't take back old garbage."

Julio blinked back a tear. "Do you enjoy hurting me?"

"Actually, yes." Shane chuckled. "Because you make it so easy. Get a spine, dude."

"Okay. How about if I call your father and tell him his favorite son is a queer fashion major."

Shane turned from a snake to a lion. "You do, and it'll

be the last call you'll ever make, Julio."

Shane passed by Taavi and Tia. He shouted so Hoss and Julio could hear him, "Play the field, Taavi. And enjoy life to the fullest—no matter who wants you or rejects you."

Julio followed him, calling out so Shane couldn't miss it, "Never believe that anyone loves you, Taavi. No matter what they tell you to get you into bed."

When the two models were in the dressing room, I hurried over to the kids. "Those guys are angry. Probably reacting to past hurts in their lives, continuing the cycle of anger and rejection."

Taavi offered me the hang loose sign. "I understand where they're coming from, Pop."

Tia added, "Thanks, Mr. Abbondanza. Taavi and I won't end up like them. I'll make sure."

"Good idea." I stood before Tia, hard at work on her machine. "Tia, thank you for helping us on the show."

Looking cute as a daisy in a canary blouse and white shorts, Tia's large dark eyes appeared from behind the sewing machine. "I love it! This place is so cool!"

A sweatshop? "I'm glad you're having a good time."

"Totally. My two favorite things are fashion and Taavi."

Taavi and Tia shared an enamored smile.

"And Tia does great work." Taavi held up a man's black leather waist pouch. "Look at what she made from Ulla's design."

And no bloody fingers. "Great work, Tia."

She blushed. "Thanks, Mr. Abbondanza." Long dark hair covered her face as she went back to work. "I take after my mother. She's an amazing seamstress." Smiling, she added, "I know it's not cool nowadays for kids to like their parents, but mine are totally the best. It sounds nerdy, but I really respect them."

"My parents are pretty cool too." Taavi grinned.

No argument there. I returned the smile. "My husband is going to invite you and your parents over for dinner later in the week. Would you like that?"

Tia looked more excited than a teenager trapped after hours in a medical marijuana station. "That is totally cool!" Again, she and Taavi shared a nod of affection.

I glanced at my watch. "Taavi, change into your second outfit. We'll start rehearsal soon."

"Sure, Pop."

"Will you excuse us, Tia?"

"Sure." Tia barely heard me, working at her machine more busily than a Mormon counting his wives.

Taavi waved. "See you later, Tia."

"Text me when you get to the dressing room," she said in teenage mode.

"I will."

I walked Taavi to the dressing room. After he texted Tia, he joined Shane and Julio in changing his clothes. Upon seeing me, Cosmo Capra hid a donut behind his back.

I stood next to him. "No worries, Cosmo. It's me, not Ulla."

Cosmo breathed a sigh of relief and sat at a makeup table. "Thanks, Professor."

Standing over him, I tried not to sound too harsh. "But you may want to ease off the snacks, at least until the show is over."

"I will, Professor."

"Thanks. Have a good rehearsal." As I left the room, I noticed Cosmo reach for a box of cookies under his chair. *He'd love my parents' bakery in Kansas.*

I continued onto the stage. When I spotted freshman fashion major Lila Hekekia and Associate Professor of Fashion Design Tyler Greenway with their heads together in the front row of the audience section, I paused behind the stage curtain and peaked out unobtrusively.

Tyler, forty-one, tall and stocky, hovered over her, his maroon sweater barely containing his bulk. "Don't be unreasonable, Lila."

"*I'm* unreasonable?" Her large dark eyes expanded like inflated balloons. "You promised me an independent study to do my own fashion show over spring break."

He ran a shaky hand through his mop of brown hair. "That was *before* Ulla Ultimate became a visiting professor and was given the slot by the dean."

"We can explain to Professor Ultimate." Lila arched her back with a determined sniff. Huge unmovable breasts descended over her tiny waist, causing her to resemble a two-way desk lamp.

Tyler's hunter green eyes hardened. "I've avoided Ulla Ultimate since she descended on Treemeadow."

"It's time you make her acquaintance."

"I've already done that." He sighed. "Ulla and I have...a past. I prefer to keep it there."

"And you and I have a present, which I don't prefer to share with the dean—unless I lose my show slot."

Ouch!

He took her small hands in his. "Lila, I could lose my job. Is that what you want?"

"I want my own fashion show, as you promised." She pulled at her braided black hair, which rested over one shoulder of her tight white dress.

"And you'll get it. One day. You're a very talented designer. But you're only a freshman."

"A freshman who was promised a show *this* semester."

Tyler begged like a dog in a steakhouse. "Can't you wait until next year?"

"I remember asking you the same question in that hotel room."

Placing a hand on her overly made-up cheek, he said, "You're so beautiful. I couldn't resist."

"I understand."

He exhaled in relief. "Good."

"Because *I* can't resist having my own show." She rose. "So, *you* need to make it happen."

Ulla Ultimate entered through the back door of theatre. She wore a black leather midriff blouse and tight black leather slacks. The fashion designer's assistant, Miles Jeffrey, walked behind her. Tyler stood faster than the EPA approving a toxic chemical. When he and Ulla were tight face to tight face, Ulla said, "Tyler Greenway. The years have left their mark on you."

"I'd say the same — if I could see past your face lift and more caked on makeup than a Geisha girl with ADD."

She glared at him. "Are you here to see my show? If so, it isn't until the end of the week."

Tyler grimaced. "Or rather *my* show."

"Or *my* show!"

Ignoring Lila, Ulla cackled like a witch in a fairy tale (*the children's kind*). "After all these years, Tyler, are you still pounding that same hollow drum?"

"Pounding and still waiting," he replied.

"For what?"

"My percentage of your income of course."

Ulla laughed so hard her platinum wig nearly slipped off. Straightening it, she said, "You'll never see a dime of my money, Tyler."

"Thanks to your high-priced lawyer."

"Thanks to the fact that my designs are originals."

He grimaced. "Can you tell me something, Ulla?"

"I'm sure I could tell you a lot of things, Tyler."

His jaw tightened. "How do you sleep at night?"

"How touching." Ulla batted her fake eyelashes. "Concerned about me getting enough rest?"

"No, I'm concerned about you stealing my designs back in college, and never paying me a dime when you became famous and I…didn't."

She folded her arms over her chest. "As I recall, when

we were in college I did your papers, and I sneaked you answers during exams."

"And in our last semester when we were partnered for the final project —"

"You slept on my lap while I created the designs."

"Created? Hardly. It was more like you traced *my* designs and then made some minor changes, thinking I wouldn't notice."

"You noticed everything about me back then." She sighed. "Until you left after graduation."

Is that a tear in her eye?

His lower lip shot out. "What did you expect me to do? You stole my work!"

"What was stolen was my heart. And when I let down my guard and told you I was ready for something more...permanent, you said you'd rather be murdered than married."

"I was twenty-one years old."

"How about now? Are you married?"

"I'm single." He sneered. "Happily."

"Perhaps time hasn't changed you at all."

Tyler winced. "What are you doing here, Ulla?"

"I'm a visiting professor with my own show." She looked him up and down. "And you?"

"I work here."

"As the custodian?"

"I'm an Associate Professor of Fashion Design."

She snickered. "Proving the old adage: those who can, do; those who can't, teach."

Says the Visiting Professor with her own fashion show.

The white makeup on her face cracked. "Tyler, since we are teaching in the same school, why is it that we haven't run into each other in this building?"

"Careful planning on my part. Refusal to attend department meetings on yours."

Lila rose and cleared her throat. "Excuse me, Professor

Ultimate. Speaking of the Fashion Department, I'm Lila Hekekia, Professor Greenway's student."

Checking out Lila's figure, Ulla sized up the situation quickly. "I'm guessing you learned a great deal 'under him.'" She turned to Tyler. "I see you still like zaftig women. At least on top. I remember your interest in my dorm roommate."

"I was never interested in her."

Ulla sighed. "Yes, 'interest' isn't the right word. How about 'hot to get her in the sack and then sack her'?"

"You still have a vile mouth, Ulla."

"And you still have a vile heart."

Lila broke in again. "Speaking of mouths, I need to speak with you, Professor Ultimate."

Ulla looked at her like the mistress of a mansion being addressed by a scullery maid. "I don't give autographs."

"No, I was—"

"My class is full, and it's far too late to register anyway."

Lila caught Tyler's attention and nodded toward Ulla.

Tyler took the not so subtle hint. "Ulla, my student is an incredibly talented designer. Do you think there might be a place for some of Lila's clothes in your show?"

"What?" the two women shrieked in unison.

"You promised me my own show!" Lila shouted.

"An Ultimate show features nothing but Ultimate fashion," Ulla replied.

Tyler added, "Don't you mean *Greenway* fashions?"

"Tell me something, Tyler." Ulla tented her fingers. "If your fashion designs are so wonderful, why haven't you developed your own line?"

He focused on the scarlet carpet and his face matched its color. "Because without anyone to stimulate and encourage me the way you did in college, I wasn't able to design anything. I spend most of the time...feeling sorry for myself."

Ulla countered with, "I thought I smelled liquor on your breath. A familiar smell as I recall."

"Yes, I drank, Ulla, after each of our dates—when you spilled alcohol down my throat to get me into bed." Tyler took a flask out of his jacket pocket and gulped down a long swig.

"And what's your excuse now?"

Lila interjected, "Can we please talk about my show?"

Before the three designers designed murder weapons, I came out (*no pun intended*) from behind the curtain, feeling like the Wizard of Oz addressing his visitors. "Everyone, we will begin rehearsal shortly."

"No, you won't."

All heads turned toward Lila.

She said, "The show must be cancelled."

Ulla rested a hand on her hip.

Better there than on Lila's throat.

"What are you talking about?" Ulla asked.

Lila stood her ground. "This slot was promised to me by Professor Greenway."

Ulla chortled. "Professor Greenway doesn't select the designers for the fashion shows at this college." She glared at him. "Or anywhere."

Lila pushed on. "The theatre isn't up to fire code."

Ulla replied, "I'll ask the dean to meet with the fire inspector and correct any violations."

Exasperated, Lila said like a religious education teacher holding a ruler, "Your show violates my religious freedom."

Ulla's jaw dropped down to her black leather necklace. "Excuse me?"

"Deuteronomy 22:5 says a woman shouldn't wear a man's garment, and a man shouldn't wear a woman's cloak."

"So?"

"So in the club scene at the activewear opening of your

show, one of the models is wearing a long black leather coat that resembles a woman's coat." Lila was on a holy roll. "And Deuteronomy 22:11 says you should not wear clothing of wool and linen mixed together."

"My clothes are made of leather," Ulla answered with a smirk.

I added, "John the Baptist wore a belt of leather."

"And look what happened to him!" Lila countered.

Thanking my comparative religions professor back in college, I pointed at Lila's braided hair, skintight white silk dress, and gold earrings. "1 Timothy 2:9-10 states that women should dress in modesty and not wear braided hair and gold, pearls, or costly clothing. Your makeup is also forbidden in the Bible." *Not to mention the affair with your professor.*

Ulla clapped her hands together like a mother superior facing a food fight in the nun's dining room. "Enough! I have no interest in books written and rewritten thousands of years ago by sexist, homophobic, bigoted men."

"What you just said violates my freedom of religion as an evangelical Christian." Lila offered Ulla a smug smile.

"You can believe whatever you like, but it has nothing to do with me."

Lila glared at her. "An evangelical judge will disagree. So your show is out, and mine is in."

Ulla looked at me with mouth agape.

I ushered Lila and Tyler toward the back door of the theatre. "My *closed* rehearsal begins in a few minutes."

Lila fumed. "You can't throw me out, Professor Abbondanza. That violates my religious freedom! I'll sue before a Republican-appointed judge—and win!"

Tyler grabbed her arm. "Let's go, Lila."

"The only place I'm going is to the dean's office!" Lila ran off.

"Wait!" Tyler glanced back at Ulla. "Thanks for your generosity and understanding."

"I learned from you twenty years ago, Tyler."

Tyler glared at her. "Twenty years and you haven't changed a bit, Ulla. You're still pathetic!" He chased after Lila.

Tears streamed down Ulla's cheeks, creating gray lines down her face.

Ulla's assistant, Miles, was at her side like a guide dog walking through city traffic on a Friday at five p.m. "Are you all right?"

She shrugged, and black leather shoulder pads brushed against her black leather earrings. "Love makes fools of us, and there's no fool like an old fool I'm afraid."

"Good morning, Mommy Dearest." Cory Ultimate, in a rainbow T-shirt and white short shorts, entered through the back door of the theatre.

Ulla turned away and wiped her face with a black leather handkerchief.

Coming between his mother and her assistant, Cory sneered at Miles Jeffrey. "And here is Mother's new henchman. Do you always dress like a frumpy businessman?"

Ulla's fists clenched. "Cory, must *you* dress like *that*?"

Cory replied, "I just put my clothes on in Shane Buff's dorm room, and now you want me to take them off again?"

Ulla glared at her son. "I meant that you could put on *more* clothes."

"You mean dress in black leather like you?"

"It's my trademark."

"And it's a fitting one—tough and cold."

Ulla threw up her hands. "Cory, will you please act your age for once. You are nineteen years old!"

"At least you know that much about me. Who my father is, what I do, if I have any problems—not so much."

She sighed. "Do we really have to play this performance again—in front of Professor Abbondanza?"

"Don't mind me. I'm accustomed to drama." *I couldn't*

resist.

Cory pointed at Miles. "You forgot to mention your latest yes-man, Mother." He sized Miles up. "Which is one thing I can't blame you for. The guy is as bland as cottage cheese on white bread."

Miles grimaced. "Are you nineteen or nine?"

"Both." Cory smirked. "Last time a guy measured me in bed."

Ulla glared at her son. "Your behavior is abominable."

Cory guffawed. "How would you know anything about my behavior, Mother? Weeks, sometimes months go by without me hearing from you."

"I have a successful fashion company to run."

"Which is clearly your top priority. I'm guessing your son is somewhere around filing your nails."

"Cory, every night before bed, I pray you are all right."

"Thoughts and prayers, Mother? Like the NRA-owned Republican legislators offer every time a lunatic guns down a herd of kids in a school?"

Miles aimed his long nose at Cory. "Why don't you give your mother a break? She works hard. And she cares about you very much."

Cory snickered. "Sure, now that I'm the technical designer and a model in her show."

Ulla cornered her son. "I would give up everything I have worked so hard for over the last twenty years if you asked me to."

He took her dare. "All right. I'm asking. Do it."

She gasped. "Who created you?"

"You and somebody I don't know."

Her eyes brimming with tears, Ulla scurried up the stairs to the runway. "I'd better check on the clothes." She disappeared backstage.

"I need to make sure the models are ready." I followed Ulla but halted behind the stage curtain and peered out coyly.

Miles shook his head, and shiny dark hair sliced the air around him. "You're quite a bad boy, aren't you?"

Cory collapsed in a front row seat. "She makes me tired."

"I'm not surprised. Your relationship with *her* seems to be all about *you*."

And the problem is? All my relationships are about me.

Cory's baby face hardened. "You don't know everything about my relationship with my mother."

"Maybe I do."

"Have you been reading her diary or her will—in bed? Do your duties include servicing my mother day and *night*?"

"You have a smart mouth. But you're missing the full picture."

Cory seethed. "Oh really?"

"Yeah, really."

"Tell me what I'm missing, Mr. Assistant?"

Miles rested his briefcase on a nearby seat. "My mother was a single working parent too. Unlike you, I wasn't an only child. As the oldest, I had to take care of three younger siblings. No after school activities, friends, or parties for me. I needed to get home and cook dinner, do laundry, clean the house, and wipe kids' bottoms. But I didn't blame my mother. I knew she was doing the best she could with the hand she was dealt."

Cory cocked his head. "What happened to your father?"

"He committed suicide." Miles plopped down into the chair next to Cory's. "After school one day, I found him in the basement with a plastic bag over his head. I was ten years old."

Poor guy.

"Why did your father do it?"

Miles sighed. "His pastor told him being gay was a sin. When marrying a woman and having children didn't 'cure him,' my father eradicated 'the sin' in the only way he had left." He laughed ironically. "I wonder what he would have thought of his gay son."

Cory did a doubletake. "You're gay?"

Miles nodded.

Another angel in Heaven gets his wings.

Cory glanced at Miles' royal blue suit. "You seem so conservative."

"Some conservatives are gay."

Cory cringed. "Are you one of those self-hating gay Republicans who try to take away my civil rights?"

"Interesting how everything becomes about you. And no, unlike my dad, I'm not a Republican. Also unlike him, I don't hate myself for being born gay."

Cory slid to the edge of his seat. "Do you think we are born gay?"

"Yes." Miles leaned back in his chair. "I assume I inherited my father's gene."

"At least you knew *your* father. My mother won't tell me anything about mine. For all I know, I could have been a test tube baby."

Miles turned toward him. "If I hadn't known my father, I'd have cherished my mother even more. One parent is better than no parents."

"Unless your one parent is the famous Ulla Ultimate."

"Your mother cares about you."

"She has an odd way of showing it."

"Ulla keeps your pictures on her desk, and she talks about you constantly."

Awwwww.

"I'm sure it's all complaints about my 'immaturity, disrespect, and wasteful life.'"

Seems about right.

Miles said, "You might be surprised."

"What do you mean?"

"Your mom brags to her business associates about your good looks, quick wit, and artistic gifts."

"To win points with her colleagues."

"I don't think so."

"Then what do you think?"

Miles smiled. "I think, like me with my mother, you're the apple of your mom's eye." He seemed far away. "My mom used to call me that. If she were still alive, I'd be all over her."

"What happened to your mother?"

His face dimmed. "She died two years ago...of neuroblastoma."

Yikes!

"What's that?"

"A type of cancer."

Cory swallowed hard. "Sorry."

"It wasn't your fault."

"I meant it must have been painful to lose a loving mother."

"It was. So you may want to think about that the next time you mouth off to yours."

"My mother and I are more complicated than that."

Miles scratched at his head. "Not that it's any of my business, but what do you have against your mother?"

Cory's body tensed. "She doesn't love me."

"You don't really believe that, Cory."

He leaned over and his pecs widened like boulders. "My childhood memories of my mother are watching her talk on the phone, work at her computer, design at her drafting table, and sew at her machine."

"So now you're punishing her for working hard to support you all those years?"

"No, she's punishing *me* for not wanting any part of her cover-up."

"Her cover-up?"

Cory nodded. "My mother is drowning herself in work, so she doesn't have to face reality."

"What reality?"

"I'm not sure. But it has to do with something that happened a long time ago. When I was a kid, I'd watch her in bed, weeping over her old diary."

Hm, a mini-mystery. Too bad we don't have a mystery solver. Wait, we do. Me!

"Did you ever ask your mom about it?"

Cory nodded. "Each time I got her cold shoulder and icy stare."

"Why don't you try to comfort her?"

"Isn't that *your* job?"

"I'm not her son. You are." Miles sighed. "I've said enough. I hope you and your mother work things out."

"I wouldn't waste too much time hoping."

"Good point." Miles opened his briefcase and took out his laptop. "My business is the task given to me by my employer."

Cory groaned. "Are you really going to be my matchmaker?"

Miles' long index finger revolved around the mousepad. "I've done quite a bit of research on the topic. A human being seems to work much more effectively than dating apps."

Cory flexed his biceps. "I don't need dating apps."

"Yes, it seems you've been quite active on campus." Miles opened a file on his computer. "So have I."

Cory cocked his head. "What do you mean?"

"I did my first interview on campus."

"You told some guy about my mother's matchmaking scheme?"

"Not exactly. I said I'm conducting a survey about gay men on campus."

"Why did he give you any information?"

"Your mother left me an expense account."

Cory gasped. "You paid someone to talk about me?"

"Pretty much."

Martin will salivate over this gossip.

Miles read from his computer screen, "Shane Buff,

twenty-one, fashion major."

"I boned him last night." Cory slid to the edge of his seat. "What did Shane say about me?"

"You don't want to know."

"You're right. He was boring in bed, and out of bed. Shane isn't right for me anyway. He's totally into himself."

Miles smirked. "Studies show opposites attract, so I agree with you there too."

Cory did a doubletake. "Did you just put me down?"

If the ego fits.

"Cory, it's pretty clear that you bedded Shane in a lame attempt at punishing your mother for not giving you the attention you crave."

"Are you a personal assistant or a psychiatrist?"

"I was a business major, but I took some psych classes in college."

"So you are psychoanalyzing me now?"

"It's not too difficult. You're a textbook example of a spoiled child crying out for affection."

Cory got to his feet. "I don't have to listen to this."

"You do if you want to hear what other guys say about you."

He resumed his seat. "I'm listening."

"After I complete more interviews, you'll be the first to know."

"I don't think you'll get very far. Most guys will play with me, but none of them want a relationship."

"You may have a point." Miles rubbed his square jaw. "Perhaps I've been going at this all wrong." He tented his fingers. "I need to get to know you better before picking a husband for you."

Cory chuckled. "I'm sure my mother had lots to say about me."

"I'd like to hear it from the source. So tell me, what don't I know about Cory Ultimate?"

Cory shrugged. "My life is pretty much an open book."

He spread his legs, revealing a huge bulge.

"I know you've been promiscuous."

Cory's eyes turned to brown slits. "Gee, feel free to say whatever you like about me, Miles."

"No problem." Miles placed his fingers on the keypad. "But I'm more interested in what *you* have to say about you."

Cory unleashed his luscious dimples. "Okay, I'm totally hot, a B student, and a terrific set and lighting designer."

Not to mention modest.

Cory smirked. "And one day I stand to inherit Ultimate Fashions, which I will sell to the highest bidder before the rest of my mother's body grows as cold as her heart."

"Why did you come to Treemeadow College?"

"It's in Vermont, and my mother lives in California."

The wonderful faculty in the Theatre Department didn't attract you?

Miles asked him, "The past murders at this college didn't frighten you?"

I solved every one of those after only five murders per case!

Cory stared at Miles defiantly. "I'm not afraid to die. Just think, when I'm dead I'll be as stiff as my mother."

"You have a smart mouth, kid."

"I was thinking the same thing about you, assistant."

Their glances met.

Cory got to his feet again. "Which reminds me. I have to check on the set before the tech rehearsal."

"Is that what you want to do with your life, be a set designer?"

He looked down at Miles. "As a matter of fact, yes."

"What draws you to the theatre?"

Your wonderful play directing professor?

Cory seemed to ponder the question. "In the theatre, it's okay to make believe, hide from the world, and create the reality of your choice. When I use my artistic skills, imagination, and technical knowledge to create a set design or a lighting plot, I feel like the master of my universe."

"Do you want to be a model too?"

"No, I'm just here for the scenery." Cory grinned.

"Then modeling seems pretty shallow."

Cory grimaced. "Since we're talking about goals, why do *you* want to be a personal assistant? That doesn't seem like a life's ambition."

"It fits my skillset."

"Creating my mother's world?"

"No, helping her navigate successfully through the world *she's* created."

Cory smirked. "How selfless."

"Not really. I take pride in Ulla's accomplishments as much as in my own."

"And you're comfortable living in my mother's shadow?"

"Just as comfortable as you are living in the shadows of a stage."

I heard footsteps behind me. So I leapt around the curtain. "Cory, please get into your wardrobe."

He saluted, leapt onto the runway, and disappeared into the dressing room. Miles sat toward the center of the house. I headed into the theatre, where I took my usual front row center seat and readied my notepad and pen. Noah sat next to me, offering a supportive hand squeeze. Martin, in a vermillion bowtie and sweater vest, and Ruben, in a matching leisure suit, filed in behind us. Craning my neck back toward Martin, I whispered, "I have some dish for you later."

He whispered back, "Forget a word of it and this campus will have another murder—yours!"

Ruben rested an arm around his husband's small back. "Leave the nice man alone, honey, so he can direct the fashion show."

Ulla Ultimate came down the runway and took a seat

next to Miles.

Finally, Hoss Packer exited down the runway, giving the illusion of a bodybuilding competition rather than a fashion show. When he was seated in the lighting booth toward the rear of the house, I called out, "Let's pick it up from where we left off last night, everyone." I noticed Associate Professor of Fashion Tyler Greenway and his student Lila Hekekia enter from the rear of the house and sit in the last row.

The house lights dimmed, and then they went on again. The stage lights came on, and they went out again.

"Hoss, is there a problem?"

"Sorry, Professor. I needed to reset the computer."

"Are you ready now, Hoss?"

He replied, "Ready."

The house lights dimmed, and the stage lights came up with a lemon glow.

"Magenta not lemon!"

"Sorry, Professor."

The stage lights turned to magenta, and the runway lights exploded — literally. After Hoss repaired them, we resumed, and the models started down the runway in their bedtime outfits. Julio Bonero was first in a black leather nightshirt and cap. At the tip of the runway, he spun into a costume malfunction — about six inches long and uncut. As I wrote a note on my pad, Cosmo Capra strutted down the runway in black leather pajamas and slippers — with chocolate stains on his cheek. When he turned, a button popped off his pajama tops. While I wrote frantically, Taavi made his appearance blowing kisses like a rock star at a concert. He smiled and strutted down the runway in black leather footed pajamas featuring pictures of animals.

After Cory showed his stuff in a long black leather T-shirt and slippers, Noah rested a hand on my knee. We said in unison, "Where's Shane?" *It's a cute couple thing we do. So is solving murder mysteries.*

When our question was met by shrugs from the models, I ran up the steps and practically flew across the runway. The dressing room was empty. Across the hall in the sewing room, I found Johnny and Tia (while texting) doing last minute repairs. "Have either of you seen Shane Buff?"

They shook their heads while they worked.

I raced out the sewing room door and scanned the area outside around the building. When I made my way toward the back alleyway, I found a bloodied Shane Buff lying motionless on the stone floor. Next to him was a mannequin streaked with blood. *Modeling for Dummies.*

Chapter Three

"When students come to this college, they should receive their dorm key and a gravestone." Detective Jose Manuello, in his fifties, wearing a dark wrinkled suit that highlighted his dark wrinkled eyes, stood next to me in the dressing room.

"I agree."

He did a doubletake that wobbled his jowls, causing him to resemble a chicken getting whiplash. "You agree with me about something, Nicky?"

"Yes. I fear for my students. With you as chief homicide detective, nobody in this town is safe." I struck my best Sherlock Holmes pose. "Thankfully the citizens of Treemeadow have *me* to solve each murder mystery and bring the culprit to justice. That's six times at Treemeadow, once in Alaska, once in Hawaii, and once in Scotland." I winked at him. "But who's keeping score?"

"You'll never score with me." Manuello laughed heartily at his own joke.

For once, I was dumbfounded. After I revived, I asked, "Did you actually make a joke, Manuello?"

He nodded proudly. "More than that, Nicky, I made a *gay* joke. See what I've learned from you?"

"I'm proud of you, Manuello." I sighed. "Now if I could only teach you how to solve a murder case." I paced à la Holmes. "And it hasn't been for lack of trying. I've given you all my knowledge and brilliant tips. To be honest, Manuello, you simply aren't a good student."

His olive cheeks turned pink. "Let's get something straight between us, Nicky."

"Is that another gay joke, Manuello?"

"No!"

"I'm so confused!" I collapsed into a chair. "Now that you're a gay humorist, it's impossible for me to know if you are joking or telling the truth."

He hovered over me. "Let me make myself clear, Nicky. *I* am the detective. You are the college theatre professor. I don't teach your classes and direct your shows, and you don't armchair detective my cases. So if you have an urge to get actively involved in this case, I want you to sit on it."

"Sit on it? Is that another gay joke?"

"Nicky!"

"I'm trying to understand you, Manuello, but with your newfound gay humor I simply don't know when you are being serious."

"How's this for serious? If you try to take over this case, I'll drop you to your knees and handcuff you."

"Is that gay humor again?"

"So help me."

"That's what I'm trying to do, but frankly I find it incredibly difficult to communicate with you now that you toss out gay jokes with more agility than one of my students texting when I write on the board."

He plopped down on the chair next to me and ran his chubby hands through his tight gray curls. "I can never win with you."

"Thank goodness you finally realized that. And after only six cases together." I put my arm around his shoulders. "Now, let's go over my case."

"*My* case."

"That's what I said." I perked up, back on the trail of a murderer. "Have your stooges taped off the crime scene area outside?"

"Yes."

"Is forensics taking samples of the area for testing?"

"Of course."

"Good."

Manuello did a doubletake. "You usually tell me, since there's such high traffic during a show, forensic testing is useless."

"It is, but it will keep your staff out of my way while I solve the case."

Manuello groaned.

"Is the body undergoing examination by the coroner?"

"Obviously. We won't release it to his parents in Kentucky until we get the report."

"Which I can give you right now."

"How can you give me the report before the coroner's examination?"

"Because I examined the body when I found him."

Manuello rose like a volcano. "Did you touch the body?"

"With my eyes only. And I can tell you how Shane Buff was murdered." Still sitting, I was at eye level with his crotch.

"A blow to the head?"

"That is incredibly offensive, Manuello?"

"Excuse me?"

"Despite your new penchant for gay humor, even in a joke, for a detective to ask me to do something like that is sexual harassment of a citizen!"

"Cut the comedy, Nicky."

"Shouldn't I be saying that to you?"

"Tell me what you have in your basket."

"Another gay joke, Manuello? Maybe you should retire, wear a rainbow shirt, and do a stand-up act in a little club in Greenwich Village, a bar in San Francisco, on the beach at Provincetown, or in the street for Mardi Gras in New Orleans."

He pulled me to my feet. "Nicky, tell me what you know about this case, or I'll grab one of the leather shirts in here and tan your hide!"

"See? You are obsessed with the humor of the gay. You mention us more than televangelists during pledge week. Though I'll admit televangelists are a great deal more comical than you."

"And they make a lot more money—tax exempt."

"But you'd look adorable in a big wig, white suit, and covered with gold jewelry.

"I'm waiting, Nicky." Manuello took a pad and pen from his inside jacket pocket.

"Haven't you graduated to a laptop yet, Manuello? My tax dollars pay for your inflated salary, medical benefits, pension, car, gas, and expense account. Surely I can also buy you a computer."

He flailed his arms like a gymnast at a bad landing. "You're lucky I don't have a laptop, Nicky, because I would slam it over your head and drag you out of town!"

"You really are a Neanderthal, Manuello."

He grabbed me by the shirt collar, face to face. "How was Shane Buff killed?"

"No matter how rough you get with me, Manuello, I will never kiss you. As you know, I'm happily married to Noah."

"Who will be a widower if you don't answer me!"

"All right, Manuello." I wriggled free and straightened my shirt and blazer. "For Noah's sake, I'll continue to share my wisdom and keen detecting skills with you. Watch and learn." I paced the room like my detective idol. "Based on the location of the blood on the mannequin and on Shane's head, it's clear that someone struck him with the mannequin."

"Why was the mannequin outside?"

"Somebody must have brought it out there."

"Who?"

I shrugged. "Everyone involved with the fashion show had access to the building, and therefore could have gone into that alleyway."

"Meaning?"

"Fashion Department faculty and students and Theatre Department faculty and students here on spring break working on the fashion show. Try to keep up, Manuello."

"Who was Shane Buff? And stand still so I don't feel like I'm in an amusement park."

I complied. "Shane was a fashion student and one of the models in our show."

"Are you and Noah modeling in the fashion show?"

I shook my head. "Just Taavi."

"How come?"

I placed my hand on my hip. "Gay jokes aren't enough? Now you want to objectify my body?"

"I don't even know what that means."

"It means that you want me up on the runway, so you can gape at my manliness as your hand disappears inside your trench coat."

"I'll make a deal with you, Nicky. I'll get a trench coat when you get some manliness."

"Is that a joke for your comedy act?"

"I'm a detective!"

"Then let me ask you something, Manuello. Does the new chief of police, who by the way is gay and married with children, know about your aspirations to perform what I believe to be a homophobic comedy routine?"

"*You* were the one who said I was performing an act."

"And it certainly isn't an act of kindness." I walked to a window and pretended to be offended.

Following me, Manuello said, "Nicky, let's start again. Tell me what you know about Shane Buff and who might want to kill him."

I pouted. "I don't think I want to answer that."

"Why?"

"Because you offended me, Manuello." I feigned tears. "And I think you should apologize—if you want me to help you with this case."

"All right." He squeezed out like a bowel movement surrounded by bleeding hemorrhoids, "I apologize."

"Very well, Manuello. But I want you to know that my feelings aren't something to toss around like your paycheck at a bar every Friday night."

"I don't drink at bars, Nicky."

I spun around. "Agh-hah! Just as I suspected. You drink at home!"

"I know what you're doing, Nicky."

"What am I doing?"

"Yanking my chain." Before I could reply, he said, "And that's not a gay joke. Neither is the gay kid who was killed."

"How did you know Shane was gay?"

"The tipped bleach blond hair, aqua contact lenses, and cut body. Besides, he was a male model."

"And there are no straight male models with tipped bleach blond hair, aqua contact lenses, and a cut body?" I scratched my head. "Actually, there probably aren't. For once we agree, Manuello."

"What else do you know about Shane Buff?"

"He was twenty-one years old, a senior fashion major."

"Who wanted him dead?"

"For two, the classmate he dumped, Julio Bonero, and the classmate he mocked for gaining weight, Cosmo Capra."

Manuello wrote on his pad. "Go on."

"My technical theatre student and set and lighting designer, Cory Ultimate, had a one-night stand with Shane. It didn't go well."

Manuello played with the rolls of fat over his belt. "Ultimate. Is he Ulla Ultimate's son?"

"A big fashion fan are you, Manuello?"

He rubbed his eyes. "I read Ulla Ultimate was doing the fashion show at the college."

"Directed by me." I bowed.

"That means your nutty friends Martin and Ruben are producing, and Noah is acting coach."

"Just like I coach *you* on how to be a detective."

"Very funny. Maybe *you* should do the stand-up act, Nicky."

"The only man I stand up to is you."

"Not Noah?"

"Noah and I make love lying down—which is none of your business."

He sat at the window seat and looked out at the green mountains surrounded by the winding crystal lake in the distance. "Let me ask you something, Nicky. Since Noah is an actor, when you two make love, do you ever think he may be faking it?"

Sitting next to him, I said, "I am going to take the high road with that question, Manuello. I won't wonder at your continued obsession with my sex life or bring up the time your wife asked Noah how to act out having an orgasm."

"She never did that."

I giggled. "You'll never know, will you, Manuello."

"Forget I asked you!"

"How could I forget your constant prying into my bedroom? Every time Noah and I make love, I think about the possibility of you popping up from underneath our bed."

"Don't think about that, Nicky."

"Then what would you like me to think about when I make love with Noah?"

Manuello groaned. "I don't care!"

"Well that says it all, doesn't it? Here I have devoted a good portion of my life to solving your murder mystery cases so you can keep your job, and you tell me you don't care about me. And now you expect me to give you information about the latest case!"

He softened. "All right. I care about you."

"Manuello, you really need to get over your feelings for me. Noah and I are monogamous."

"Did Ulla Ultimate have a motive to kill Shane Buff?"

"No need to shout, Manuello. Unlike you, I'm still in my prime and can hear quite well, thank you."

"Nicky!"

"All right. I hate to see you so on edge. It can't be good for someone so overweight and sedentary."

He clenched his fists. "I'm warning you, Nicky."

"Have we come to this, Manuello? That you are actually threatening me with violence?"

"Yes. Now talk." He readied his pad and pen.

"As always, your wish is my command. Ulla wasn't too pleased about her son's sexual proclivities. She hired her personal assistant to find Cory a husband."

Manuello wrote as he mumbled, "Go on."

"Shane made an uncompleted pass at Hoss Packer, my hunky theatre student stage manager, which for some reason upset Johnny Riley, an accident-prone fashion design major."

"Is that all?"

"Well, an uncompleted pass may not be a big deal to you, since you've made so many at me, but for some people it can be an issue."

"Would somebody murder someone for it?"

"To be honest, I've thought about it a few times, Manuello."

He moaned. "Are those all the suspects?"

"There may be two more."

"Who?"

"Fashion design student Lila Hekekia might have taken her frustrations out on Shane."

"Meaning?"

"Lila's insatiable desire for her *own* spring fashion show, as promised to Lila by Associate Professor of Fashion Design Tyler Greenway, could have resulted in her killing one of Ulla's models."

"Is that everyone who was in or around the fashion building today?"

"No. But of course Noah, Martin, and Ruben didn't commit the murder."

He smirked. "That's true. If Noah hasn't murdered you after all these years, and Martin and Ruben haven't murdered each other, they'd never kill anyone."

"Save that for your act, Manuello." I added, "And Taavi and Tia Tedesco were here, but I would hardly consider my son and his girlfriend suspects."

"Taavi has a girlfriend?"

I nodded. "So he won't be able to be fodder for your gay act."

Manuello rubbed his lined forehead. "How does that work?"

"Heterosexuality? If you don't know, *I* certainly can't help you."

"I mean when two gay dads have a straight kid?"

"I guess the same way it works when a mom and dad have a gay kid."

"How is that?"

"Hopefully the parents love and support their child."

He slid to the edge of his seat. "So you and Noah are okay with Taavi being straight?"

"Of course."

"I'm surprised."

I cocked my head. "You're surprised we love our son and want him to be happy?"

"I assumed you would want Taavi to be gay."

"We want Taavi to be whatever he is inside."

"Hm."

"Manuello, do you think Noah and I are bigots?"

"No, but you both seem really into the gay thing."

"Says the man who is rehearsing a stand-up act on gay life."

"I'm not doing that!"

"Then are you preparing to do your comedy act on a gay TV network?"

He closed his pad. "We're done here. I asked everyone to wait in the theatre house."

"So I can resume my technical rehearsal?"

"No. That's cancelled for the day."

"What about my show?"

"It's still on—for the time being. Now send each person in here one at a time for questioning."

"Shouldn't we reverse roles?"

"I'm not going to be your go-fer, Nicky!"

"That's probably a good idea, given how out of shape you are, Manuello." I leapt to my feet. "I'll bring in each suspect for us to interview."

He replied to my back, "I'm interviewing them alone!"

Pretending I didn't hear him, I entered the theatre. Noah met me at the edge of the runway. "Noah, can you walk Martin and Ruben to their car? And promise Martin I'll tell him everything later."

"Of course." Noah took my hand. "Are you all right?"

"I am now."

Taavi appeared at Noah's side. "Case number ten, Pop! Should I interview everyone?"

"You should get into your dad's car, so he can drive Tia and then you home." *Hopefully slower than a spacecraft launching.* I kissed their cheeks. "I'll see you both later."

"Be careful, Nicky."

"Always."

"Call if you need my help, Pop!"

I brought our first interviewee into the dressing room. Once Julio Bonero was seated at a makeup table near the door, Manuello and I sat opposite him on a loveseat (*feeling anything but loving*).

Julio, still in his black leather nightshirt from the show, obviously watched too many television police dramas. "Am I under arrest, Detective?"

Manuello raised a gray eyebrow. "This is an interview."

I explained, "Just tell the detective everything you know. And don't forget to mention that you and Shane were involved, Shane broke things off, and you threatened to tell his father that Shane was a gay fashion major rather than a straight business major."

Manuello scowled at me. "May I speak with Mr. Bonero?"

"Of course." I waved Manuello on and sat back on the loveseat.

Manuello asked, "Mr. Bonero, when was the last time you saw Shane Buff alive?"

"About fifteen minutes before I came onto the runway at the tech rehearsal." Julio blinked back tears. "Shane and I had been talking."

"About what?" I asked, followed by a threatening glance from Manuello.

Julio slumped down in his seat. "I wanted to try again with Shane, and I told him so."

"And?"

Manuello nudged my side.

"Shane wasn't interested. He slipped out the back dressing room door for some air."

I asked, before Manuello stepped on my foot, "Did you go after him?"

"Yes."

"What happened?"

"I told him I missed him, and I pleaded for another chance at our relationship. Shane mocked me and said he'd never go back to 'slumming it.' Not wanting him to see me cry, I ran back into the dressing room. Ten minutes later when I entered the stage, I assumed Shane was behind me.

With his ego, Shane would never miss a cue." Julio swallowed hard. "But he missed that one."

Manuello asked, "Were you angry with Shane for breaking up your relationship?"

"Yeah. I couldn't stand to see him with other guys."

"Why is that?" I asked.

"Because I was totally in love with the dude, but clearly he wasn't in love with me."

Manuello said, "That's all...for now."

Julio glanced at him. "Can I ask you a question?"

Manuello nodded.

"Have you ever worked on a television crime show?"

Manuello sighed. "I'm a detective, not an actor."

Julio nodded. "But I read somewhere that television cop shows hire detectives to read the scripts and be on the set — to make sure everything is done authentically."

Manuello replied in a deadpan, "I've never done that."

"Maybe you should."

"Why?"

"To help a Treemeadow student get a role on a TV show."

Cosmo Capra was next on the witness stand. *Or rather the makeup chair.*

"Cosmo, how did you feel when Shane mocked your weight?"

Manuello showed me his molars.

"It hurt." Cosmo pushed a cookie further down the pocket of his black leather pajamas.

"Where were you when Shane Buff was murdered?" Manuello asked.

Cosmo asked, "What time was that?"

I replied, "About ten minutes before the models entered the stage for the technical rehearsal."

Cosmo's full face reddened. "I was outside in the alleyway with Shane."

"Why?" Manuello asked.

"I had hidden a box of cookies in the alley. When I went to retrieve it, Shane called me a name."

"What name?"

"'Mondo model.'" Cosmo hung his head. "It means 'fat.'"

"Did you two have it out?" Manuello asked.

Cosmo nodded. "I told him to lay off me or he'd be sorry. Then I hurried back into the dressing room."

"Was Shane alive when you left him?" I asked.

Cosmo nodded, and the cookie fell out of his pocket.

Next, the makeup chair barely contained Hoss Packer's bulk.

Before Manuello could open his mouth, I said, "Hoss, where were you before you entered the theatre for the tech rehearsal today?"

Hoss's abdominal muscles expanded and contracted under his tight T-shirt. "I was out in the alley behind the dressing room—bringing in a new piece of lighting equipment."

Manuello countered with, "Did you see Shane Buff out there?"

"Our paths crossed."

Probably like metal to a magnet. "Did Shane make a pass at you?"

Hoss looked away. "I don't like telling tales about dudes out of school."

"We're *in* school, and the dude is deceased."

"All right, Professor." His dark eyes widened. "Shane threw himself at me. And it wasn't the first time. Or the second. I told him I'd had enough. He said he'd never get enough—of me. I showed my fist and warned him to stay away. Then I trekked back inside."

Manuello asked, "Did you hit Shane Buff before you entered the dressing room."

"No, but I wanted to."

Johnny Riley sat with his bandaged hand on his

bandaged knees.

"Johnny, why did you get upset and leave when Hoss spoke to you earlier in the sewing room?"

"I'd rather not say, Professor." He glanced down at the blood stain on his jeans.

Manuello asked, "Is that *your* blood, Mr. Riley?"

He nodded. "I've been working on some alterations for the clothes in the show."

"Sewing with knives, are you?"

I explained, "Johnny is having some difficulty with the leather fabric."

"And he's obviously also having some difficulty with Hoss Packer."

"No!" Johnny raised his bandaged palm to his mouth. "It's not that."

I interceded. "Did it upset you when Shane came on to Hoss?"

"Sort of." Johnny squirmed in his seat.

Clearly attributing Johnny's discomfort to puppy love for Hoss, Manuello asked, "Mr. Riley, where were you before the rehearsal, when Shane Buff was in the alleyway behind the building?"

"Next to Shane."

Manuello perked up. "Why?"

"I had tried to widen a buttonhole on a jacket, and I cut a piece of my thumb off with a scissors. After bandaging it—my thumb, not the scissors—I thought some fresh air might help it heal—my thumb, not the scissors."

"Did you speak with Shane Buff?"

Johnny nodded, and fly-away auburn hair surrounded him like a halo. "Shane asked me a question."

"What question?" Manuello and I asked in unison.

"Shane asked me, 'How can someone be such a completely repugnant nerd?'"

Manuello held his hand over my mouth. "What did you answer, Mr. Riley?"

"I told Shane that throwing himself at others was pretty repugnant too. Shane said not to worry, since he'd never throw himself at a 'gross dweeb' like me. Having enough fresh air and more clothes to alter, I went back inside."

Our next interview was with Lila Hekekia.

Clearly noticing Lila's enormous assets, Manuello struggled to lift his gaze from her chest to her eyes. "Ms. Hekekia, do you have a problem with Ulla Ultimate's fashion show?"

"Yes."

"Why?"

"The time slot was originally promised to me by Professor Greenway, my fashion designs are better than Professor Ultimate's, and when I pray about it, God tells me he's on my side."

"God speaks to you?" he asked.

"Yes, when I pray. And when I read the Bible, which clearly states in Leviticus that two men shall not lie together."

I couldn't resist. "The correct translation is a man and a *boy* should not lie together."

Manuello shooed me away. "Ms. Hekekia, what does that have to do with Ulla Ultimate's fashion show?"

Lila explained with the diligence of a fracker injecting toxic chemicals into the ground, "Professor Ultimate's models and their wardrobe celebrate the homosexual lifestyle."

I don't own any leather. Does that excommunicate me from the gay club?

She tugged at the hem of her form-fitting white dress. "That kind of display has led to same-sex so-called marriage, which deeply affects me and my upcoming marriage."

"If same-sex marriage affects your upcoming heterosexual marriage, then you or your husband-to-be must be gay."

Manuello kicked my shin. "Are you engaged, Ms. Hekekia?"

"No, but I will be one day. And what kind of a marriage will I have knowing marriages of sin surround my marriage approved by God?"

My gander raised to the cracked ceiling. "If same sex marriage is forbidden, why isn't Jesus quoted as saying that in the Bible stories?"

She raised her dark eyes to her fake eyelashes. "Probably because Jesus was so busy healing the sick, feeding the hungry, clothing the naked, and serving everyone. I believe that's the message of the New Testament: Doing those things Jesus did will only get you crucified. Better to fend for yourself and let the less fortunate deal with their own mess."

Manuello stopped taking notes. "Ms. Hekekia, did you have anything against Shane Buff?"

"Only that he was a model in Professor Ultimate's show, which should be *my* show. As I mentioned, Professor Greenway promised me an independent study show over spring break."

"Did you see Shane Buff before the technical rehearsal?"

She nodded. "Tyler...Professor Greenway and I had words outside the theatre. I ran away from him, around the building, smack into Shane."

"Did you and Shane Buff have words too?"

"Yes."

Manuello said, "I'm guessing they weren't pleasantries."

She played with a gold earring. "I told Shane that Professor Ultimate's fashion show was religious discrimination against me. He called me a clown."

Gazing at her thick makeup, I didn't blame Shane.

Lila added, "I said I would pray that he burns forever

in the dark recesses of Hell, which it seems I've done quite successfully." She smiled sweetly. "Never underestimate an evangelical's power of prayer, Detective."

Associate Professor of Fashion Design Tyler Greenway scratched at his chestnut-colored hair and barrel chest as he corroborated Lila's story. "When I got to alleyway, Lila had already gone. Shane was pretty steamed, mouthing off about Lila. I told him to can it, and he started in on *me*."

Manuello asked, "Did you and Mr. Buff come to blows."

I winked at Manuello and he shot me a threatening gawp.

Tyler explained, "I'd already failed Shane in my class for his bad attitude and lazy work ethic. I told him what a useless piece of garbage he was, and then I made my way around the building and back inside the theatre to find Lila and watch the rehearsal."

Cory Ultimate's baby brown eyes stared at us next. "Shane was a notch on my bedpost. Nothing more."

Manuello asked, "Do you have many notches there, Mr. Ultimate?"

Cory smiled at his crotch. "When you got it, flaunt it."

"Did it bother you that Shane wasn't interested in a second notch?" I asked.

"Hardly." Cory sniffed. "Shane didn't appreciate a good thing when he had it."

"Did you tell him that?" Manuello asked.

"As a matter of fact, I did. Just before the rehearsal started. I found him in the alleyway behind the dressing room."

Manuello and I shared a glance. He asked, "What was Mr. Buff's reaction."

"Shane told me to go screw myself, which I said I'd rather do than have another boring night with him."

Miles Jeffrey pulled back the broad shoulders filling out his blue suit. "After Cory disappeared, Ulla asked me to go outside and make sure he was all right. I checked around the building and didn't find him. Instead I came upon Shane Buff in the alley behind the dressing room."

Manuello wrote a note. "Did you and Mr. Buff share words?"

Miles chuckled. "Hardly. Shane asked if I'd like a quickie with him behind a tree. When I declined by saying, 'I'm not a dog,' he called me a 'bitch.' I'd had enough of his insanity, and I went back inside the theatre."

Ulla Ultimate lifted her surgically tight white face and adjusted a strand of hair in her platinum wig. "I'm always jittery before a tech rehearsal of one of my fashion shows. Taking a walk generally calms me down." Her violet eyes flashed anger. "Until today when I came upon Shane Buff behind the fashion building. He told me he should be featured as the star model in my show. When I declined, he said my son was a 'bad lay.' I wanted to strangle him with one of my spiked dog collars."

"Did you?" Manuello asked, pen in hand.

Ulla came to. "No. I went back inside to see the rehearsal of my show."

When Manuello and I were alone, he rested his head in his hands. "Nine suspects, all with motive, each with access, and none with alibis."

"Cheer up, Manuello." I patted his creaky knee. "My 'little gray cells' haven't failed me yet. Go back to your job giving parking tickets, or whatever it is you do on my tax dollars, and let the professional handle this."

Before he could commit a second murder, I hurried out of the room, through the theatre, and out the back door. The late afternoon sun surrounded the campus in a golden glow. Hearing my stomach growl louder than a dog meeting a new mail carrier, I ducked into the cafeteria and ate a turkey avocado club sandwich on eight-grain bread with a spinach cucumber carrot juice. Recharged, I headed for the gym, where my legs and lungs rebelled on the treadmill and elliptical, and my shoulders and back turned a cold shoulder to me in the weight room. Then realizing I left my notes in the fashion theatre, I dragged my sore body back to the fashion building.

Encircling the rectangular white stone edifice, I noticed the yellow tape remained in the alleyway behind the dressing room, but the police had gone. I walked back around and entered the theatre through the rear door, again basking in the dark place I called home. Suddenly, a beautiful figure all in white floated onto the stage. Her whitish blonde hair resembled fluffy clouds. She spun gracefully, the floor-length white satin dress enveloping her like wings. As I hid in the rear of the darkened theatre, I marveled at her beauty, grace, and ephemeral aura. When she glided down the runway in my direction, I exited out the back door.

A bit spooked, I called Noah on my cell phone, told him about it, and asked him to pick me up. We arrived at our Victorian home faster than a conservative political group taking over social media accounts to distribute fake news during an election.

After dinner (grilled Peruvian chicken with new potatoes and prune-sweetened lacinato kale), I went over my notes and answered emails in the upstairs study. Then I met up with Noah on opposite sides of Taavi's sleigh bed. I moved a clump of hair off our son's forehead. "Are you all right with what happened at the theatre today?"

"Not really, Pop."

Noah and I shared a worried glance.

"Shouldn't *I* be the first model on the runway for the nightwear? And why didn't you let me help you interview the suspects in the case?"

That's our boy. "Taavi, there's only one director on this show, and it's me."

"Tia says I should be the first model out."

"If Tia wants to negotiate with me on your behalf,

she'll need an agent's license."

"I should get a private investigator's license." Taavi pouted.

Noah tucked the white sheet under his chin. "Murder isn't child's play. It's serious business."

"I know, Dad! That's why I examined the place where Shane was killed, and I snooped around everyone's conversations."

"You shouldn't be doing that."

"You do it all the time, Pop."

Good point. "Get some sleep. We have rehearsal again tomorrow."

"I'm guessing there'll be another murder tomorrow."

Noah's handsome face registered concern. "Does that upset you, Taavi?"

"Yes!" Taavi looked giddier than a teacher in late June. "Unless you guys let me help you solve the mystery!"

Noah and I each kissed a cheek. Taavi reached for the laptop in a drawer under his bed."

"What are you doing?" Noah asked.

"Skyping with my grandparents before bed." Taavi sat up and rested the laptop on his knees. "It relaxes me when I'm doing a show."

"Which grandparents?" I asked.

"Both of them."

I rose. "Give them our love."

"And don't stay up too late." Noah was behind me.

I shut the door as we left the room.

When Noah and I were naked under our fifteen thousand thread count white satin sheets in our fourposter, I lay on my back and gazed at the sea-blue walls surrounding us like clear sky.

Noah cuddled into my chest. "I'm glad Taavi has a close relationship with our parents."

"Me too." I kissed the top of his head.

He gazed up at me. "Were you close to your

grandparents?"

"My parents took my brother and me to visit them in Italy a few times. I remember them feeding Tony and me until we got sick to our stomachs. They're gone now. How about you?"

"My mom's parents are in a nursing home back in Wisconsin. She visits every weekend. When I was a kid, I remember them as warm, loving, and doting. Sadly, they've been suffering from dementia for most of my adulthood. I never knew my dad's parents."

"How come?"

"They passed away very young."

"How sad. Of what?"

A crease formed on Noah's smooth forehead. "My grandma died in childbirth. My grandpa died of lymphoma. My dad was a boy, sharing the bathroom with his father when his dad found the lumps on his neck, underarms, and groin. It was obviously tragic for them both. My grandfather went pretty quickly. He was only thirty-five."

Noah's age.

"Life is full of joys and sorrows." He kissed my chest. "As proven by my wonderful husband who is a joy, and yet another murder mystery full of sorrow."

"You'd think by now we'd be accustomed to it."

"Murder is never ordinary, or easy."

I kissed his soft cheek and smelled strawberries.

Always concerned about others, Noah said, "I hope the members of our cast and crew are all right."

I came to the point (*in more ways than one since my erection lifted the sheet*). "Since nobody else is on campus during spring break, a member of our cast and crew is the murderer."

Noah sighed. "And if history repeats itself, which it often does, Shane's won't be the only murder."

"And Manuello will be as ineffective as ever."

He kissed my nose. "That's why Treemeadow is lucky to have its own Sherlock Holmes."

I kissed his neck. "And John Watson." Moving into director mode, I said, "Speaking of Shane, I need to find a replacement for him in the show."

"No other students are on campus now."

I grinned. "So a faculty member will have to fill Shane's tight leather outfits."

"Who?"

"Let's see. We need someone handsome, with a hot body, and charisma to die for. A guy Shane's size." I lay on top of him. "Look! I just found someone."

Noah's eyes filled with moisture. "You think I'm still good looking enough to be a model?"

"No. I don't think it. I *know* it." We shared a long, wet kiss. "Come here, sexy runway boy."

"Why, Mr. Director!"

"I have an idea." Racing into the bathroom, I grabbed my new skin cream. Hurrying back into bed, I waved it in front of Noah's face. "Let's smother our bodies in this."

"Kinky!"

I rubbed the cream all over Noah's gorgeous body, and he reciprocated. Then I licked from his sweet face down his soft neck and chest to his tight stomach. When I reached his mound of gold, I took his long, thin, curved manhood into my mouth. It smelled of flowers and felt like velvet. Noah writhed and moaned in appreciation. Then I flipped him over to his side and spooned him. Upon entering the man of my dreams, Noah cried out in grateful appreciation. We built up a steady rhythm of love until I reached out for him. Moments later we both screamed our orgasms and then rested in each other's arms. Just before sleep overtook me, I thought about the ghost in the theatre and wondered if she had something to do with Shane Buff's murder.

I woke the next morning with the suspects' voices in my head. Anxious to get back to the fashion theatre for the show — and to solve the mystery — I showered, slathered my body with the new skin cream, dressed, and raced downstairs. Noah, Taavi (cell phone to Tia in hand), and I ate breakfast — ricotta stuffed whole wheat French toast with berries — at the kitchen nook. Then Noah and Taavi cleaned up while I downed my vitamins with an apple cucumber ginger smoothie. Finally, Noah sped us to the campus faster than Aladdin on his carpet — with the movie playing on fast forward.

We entered the Fashion Department theatre from the back door. Ulla Ultimate, in a black leather tube top and mini skirt was in heated battle with Associate Professor of Fashion Tyler Greenway, his stocky build stuffed inside a gold sweater and black slacks. Standing opposite her in the aisle, Tyler asked, "Ulla, even one outfit?"

"No."

"A guest spot?"

"Tyler, just like I told you back in college when you asked me if one of your...dalliances could copy my homework, the answer is 'never.'"

"But Lila's designs are really good."

"Unfortunately, your designs on her aren't." Ulla clutched at his wide arm. "Let me give you some advice, Tyler. Don't touch what you teach."

He fumed. "I'm a tenured associate professor. You're a visiting professor. I hope your visit is short and sweet."

"Like our relationship in college?"

He grimaced. "I'd have stuck around longer if you'd have paid more attention to me."

She laughed ironically. "Being called a thief by one's boyfriend somehow kicks the crap out of a relationship. Not to mention your constant declarations of independence and revulsion for any type of commitment."

His eyes narrowed. "Listening to you now, Ulla, it's clear I made the right decision back then."

Ulla turned away.

Lila Hekekia entered from the rear door. She wore a form-fitting silver lowcut blouse and short skirt. Sauntering up to Ulla, the fashion student said, "Professor Ultimate, do I get my show?"

Ulla offered the girl an icy stare. "What you get is the hell out of my tech rehearsal."

Lila nudged Tyler.

He rested his head in his hands. "You're making a mistake, Ulla. This young woman has talent."

"I'm sure." Ulla smirked.

Lila clutched at her silver necklace. "Professor Ultimate, if I don't get my own show, I will be suing you, Professor Greenway, and the college for breaking a promise to me."

Ulla let out a guttural laugh. "Good luck with that, honey."

Lila fired back with, "And I will be suing the college for religious discrimination against me."

Ulla guffawed. "By what law book?"

"God's law — the Bible!"

Since Ulla, Lila, and Tyler didn't seem to realize there was an audience for their battle, I followed Noah and Taavi up the stairs and across the runway. Seasoned model Taavi took novice Noah by the hand and led him to the dressing room. I paused at the flat upstage, where Cory Ultimate, silver paint in hand, was touching up the painted chains hanging in the dungeon. "Nice work, Cory."

"Thanks, Professor." His lime tank top and canary short shorts highlighted his gym body.

Spotting Julio Bonero coming from the dressing room, I said, "Julio, I'm sorry for your loss. I know you and Shane were...friends."

Julio's long dark hair covered his face.

Probably to mask the tears in his eyes.

Julio said, "I didn't sleep much last night, Professor. I still can't believe Shane is gone. Why would anyone want to kill Shane?"

Resting a hand on Julio's sculpted shoulder, I said, "That's what I'm going to find out."

Cory placed his hand on Julio's other shoulder. "Want to cry on my pillow?"

Julio twitched him away like a mosquito during a West Nile virus outbreak. "Have some respect for Shane's death, man."

"Oh, I do." Cory pinched Julio's bottom. "But I have more respect for your bubble butt."

"You're a pig."

"True." Cory smiled. "But I'm a pig with connections in television land."

"You're delusional, dude."

"Maybe, but I have a famous mother."

Julio seemed to have second thoughts. "Can you really get me hooked up with TV producers?"

"Let's you and me hook up first."

Julio backed away. "You're just yanking my chain, man."

"Not yet. But I will be soon."

Julio glanced out at Ulla Ultimate, now seated in the center of the house. "You don't know anyone in television. You're acting out to spite your mother."

Ulla Ultimate glared at her son from the audience section.

Julio added, "Why did I waste my time talking to you?"

Hoss Packer entered the stage to refocus a light. Cory, after checking to make sure his mother was still watching, wrapped his arms around Hoss's V-shaped back — housed in a tight salmon-colored T-shirt complimenting Hoss's dark skin. Cory looked more excited than a priest surrounded by altar boys at his ordination. "Here's my sexy stallion stage manager."

Try saying that three times fast while riding a horse.

He massaged Hoss's back muscles. "As a model, my ideal weight is you on top of me."

Julio pushed Cory away from Hoss. "Get off him!"

Cory regrouped. "Why, Julio? Now that your ex has marked the spot, do you want Hoss as your new conquest?"

"Professor, I finished Taavi's new hat for—" Johnny Riley appeared, stopped in his tracks, glanced at Hoss, and then ran back to the sewing room.

Hoss glared at Julio and Cory. "I'm not interested in either of you two guys. Will you both get that through your heads?" Then Hoss followed Johnny, and I followed Hoss.

When I reached the sewing room, I pretended to watch Tia and Taavi at Tia's work station as I glanced over at Johnny and Hoss.

Behind his sewing machine, Johnny sat still in a white T-shirt and jeans that hung off him like branches on a willow tree.

Hoss stood over Johnny like Gulliver in Lilliput. "Have I done something to offend you?"

Johnny shook his head, and a cyclone of red enveloped him.

"Do I upset you?"

Johnny shook his head again and the bandage on his forehead slid down covering his eyes.

Hoss replaced the bandage. "You're going to get yourself killed if you keep working in here."

Johnny lifted his shirt and revealed a large bandage on his flat stomach. "When I was steaming fabric, I bumped into the steamer." He pointed to a large open vat-like structure in a corner of the room.

"Are you that accident prone?"

"I guess I'm just not into leather."

They shared a laugh.

Hoss sat on the edge of the work table opposite Johnny's sewing machine. I feared it would tip over. "I'd like to be friends."

Johnny swallowed, and his large Adam's apple wobbled like a yo-yo. "That's nice of you to say."

"It's not nice. It's the truth."

"I don't think so." Johnny rose and headed toward a fabric cabinet in the corner of the room.

Hoss blocked his path. "I don't lie."

"But I do. And you know it." Johnny's face was filled with admiration. "Hoss, you're an attractive, honest, sweet, strong, hard-working, talented, wonderful person, and I'm…not. So you don't have to pretend to like me. You deserve a friend who isn't a phony." He ran into the bathroom.

Julio entered the sewing room and made his way over to Hoss. "What Cory said out there was rude. But it was also true. I was totally bummed about what happened to Shane. Now I realize you're a terrific guy, much more my style than Shane ever was. I know you don't want to date me, but do you think we could hook up sometime?"

Hoss ran a hand through his short dark hair. "I don't think that's a good idea, Julio."

"Why not?"

"I'm flattered that you like me, but we're really different people."

"Meaning you're better than me, dude?"

"Meaning it would never work out between us. So let's concentrate on the show."

Julio's handsome face contorted into a monstrous mask. "Thanks for giving me a shot, Hoss. I hope you're happy with your clumsy friend, Johnny. That is, if he has any fingers left to jerk you off." Then he added, "By the way, do you know anyone in the television industry?"

"No!"

"Figures." As Julio passed Taavi, Tia, and me, he called out over his shoulder toward Hoss, "Immerse yourself in your career, Taavi. Love isn't worth the trouble."

Cosmo entered the sewing room from the dressing room.

Julio breezed by him. "Cosmo, do you have any television contacts?"

Cosmo shrugged. "I eat in front of the TV screen a lot." He bit into a ham sandwich.

Julio groaned. "How appropriate that the pig is eating his own kind." He strutted to the dressing room.

In the awkward silence that followed, I said to Cosmo, Hoss, Taavi, and Tia, "Julio is upset over what happened to Shane. I'm sure we are all quite shaken."

Cosmo nodded, eating his sandwich. Then he turned to Hoss. "As a bodybuilder, do you have a special diet?"

Hoss nodded. "Protein every two hours."

"Care to share that diet with me sometime?"

Hoss shrugged his mountainous shoulders. "Sure. I'll give you my workout routine if you like too."

"No, thanks. Just the diet." Cosmo asked, "Can we chat for a bit after the show?"

Johnny came out of the bathroom, gasped, and ran into the dressing room. Hoss followed him.

Oblivious, Cosmo reached for a box of cookies hidden in the open cabinet behind tall spools of thread. When Taavi and Tia noticed, Cosmo placed the cookies in front of them. "Don't let anyone ever tell you not to eat, Taavi. Eat as much as you like, whatever you like, and as often as you like. Promise me you'll do that?"

Eyeing the cookies, Taavi nodded.

Then Cosmo lifted a costume hanging from a rack and ate the sandwich as he walked back to the dressing room.

I admired Tia's work. "Love the leather belt, Tia."

Her face lit up like a torch at a luau. "Thank you, Mr.

Abbondanza. I've started to think about designing my own show someday."

Taavi beamed with pride, between bites of a cookie. "Tia has some great ideas about our futures, Pop."

Hopefully they will entail physical therapy for carpal tunnel syndrome from texting. Admiring her paisley blouse and buttercup shorts, I asked, "Did you make the clothes you're wearing?"

She continued working. "My mom made them."

"I can see where you get your talent."

"Yeah. My dad is pretty amazing too."

I asked, "Does he sew?"

Tia giggled. "He's a businessman."

"We're looking forward to all of us getting together for dinner soon."

"That will be so cool!" they both said.

Taavi and Tia do it too!

Taavi took Tia's hand (*his other hand free for more cookies*), and they gazed at each other adoringly.

I headed back to the stage, slipping behind the curtain to watch Cory Ultimate in whispered conversation with his mother's assistant, Miles Jeffrey. "How's the matchmaking business going, Miles?"

Miles opened a file on his laptop. "I interviewed Julio Bonero, twenty-one, fashion major."

"I'm not interested in Julio."

"Then why were you flirting with him?"

"Why do you think?"

"Congratulations. Your scheme worked. Your mother wasn't pleased. Did you bed Julio too?"

Cory placed a hand on his hip. "Are you my matchmaker or my conscience?"

"Is there a difference?"

He groaned. "Julio and I never moved beyond the flirting stage."

Martin will be disappointed.

Miles closed the file. "Julio isn't interested in you

either. Strike two." He looked up from his computer. "It's not easy trying to find a good mate for you."

"It's also not easy being Ulla Ultimate's son."

"I imagine it's not a piece of cake being Cory Ultimate's mother either."

"You have a lot of smart answers for an assistant."

"You have a lot of smart answers for someone who takes his mother's money."

Cory did a doubletake. "How do you know about that?"

"I write the checks."

Cory sobered. "I appreciate the things my mother has done for me."

"Then why not act like it? She won't be around forever. Take it from one who knows."

When they spotted me entering the stage, Cory scooted to the dressing room, and Miles hurried to his seat in the center of the theatre next to Ulla. I called for everyone's attention and delivered a Tony Award-worthy dramatic tribute to Shane Buff—using lots of tissues and talent. Then I announced Noah as Shane's replacement. Finally, I asked everyone to pick up where we had left off the day before.

Once I was seated front and center, Martin whispered from behind me, "You have some 'splaining' to do, my friend."

I nodded. "I'll tell you everything I know soon."

Next to Martin, Ruben said, "I certainly hope so, Nicky. He's been up at night asking so many questions it's disturbing my sleep."

Martin retorted, "A rock band playing for a senior citizen audience couldn't disturb your sleep."

I called out, "Can we begin?"

The house lights turned to purple, and the stage lights went off.

"Hoss!"

"Sorry, Professor!" Hoss reversed the lighting cue and

the models entered the runway in their casualwear. Taavi was first, though I didn't stage it that way (*Grrr!*), looking adorable in a black leather polo shirt and shorts. He strutted down the runway waving the black leather cap Johnny had just finished making for him. Next was Noah looking incredibly sexy in a black leather jumpsuit. As he turned and posed, Noah seductively twirled a black leather scarf that made my pants tighten. Cory Ultimate truly embodied the Ultimate fashion in a black leather kilt. Reaching the lip of the runway, he lifted his kilt and blew a kiss at Hoss. Ulla groaned, and I wrote more threats on my notes than a teacher on a first quiz. Then Cosmo Capra ambled out in a black leather shirt, slacks, and buttoned blazer. When he spun at the end of the runway, buttons popped, the blazer opened, and candy spilled from the jacket pockets like hand grenades. I wrote notes until my hand ached.

Ulla marched down the aisle and whispered in my ear, "The chubby model has to go, Nicky."

"I'll deal with it, Ulla."

Lila was next at my other ear. "The Bible says gluttony is a sin, Professor. I'll be mentioning that foodaholic model in my religious discrimination lawsuit."

Tyler Greenway pulled Lila away, but not before whispering in my ear, "The chubby guy was trouble in my class. He wouldn't observe my 'no eating in class' policy, and he confronted me on it in front of all the other students."

"Can we please finish the rehearsal!"

Tyler, Lila, and Ulla went back to their seats.

There was a pause onstage. My heart skipped a beat. Then another. Noah and I made frightened eye contact. Taavi looked hopeful. I leapt up to the runway and sprinted to the dressing room. After searching all over, I found Julio Bonero lying behind a changing screen. Next to his bloody neck was an equally bloody sheering scissors. *Cut!*

CHAPTER FOUR

An hour later, Martin, Ruben, Noah, Taavi, and I sat on tall leather chairs next to the cherry fireplace mantel in Martin's office. Noah and Taavi had changed back into their street clothes. Martin wore a lavender bowtie and sweater vest, and Ruben sported a matching leisure suit. It felt like home in our department head's office in the theatre building as Martin served us hot cocoa and finger sandwiches on fine china. Martin's administrative assistant, Shayla Johnson, as usual listened to our every word from her perch at the desk in the outer office.

Martin rested a lavender monogramed napkin on his small lap. "Two down, three murders to go before you solve another case, Nicky."

Ruben wiped the corner of his mouth with his napkin. "Is Manuello threatening to close down our fashion show? We've invited a lot of people, and Ulla Ultimate has covered all the expenses."

"I can take care of Manuello," I replied.

"Where is he?" Noah asked.

"I left him at the fashion theatre, gazing dimly at the body and scissors, and botching up interviews with suspects. That should keep him out of my hair for a while." I rested my cup and plate on a cherry end table. "On the positive side, we're down to only eight suspects."

Shayla called out, "As usual they all had motive, no alibi, and easy access to the dressing room of the fashion theatre. Now hurry up and get to the juicy stuff. I don't work overtime."

Martin shot me dagger eyes. "Yes, give me all the dirt, Nicky. And not behind the ears, but in the bedroom."

I was as obedient as a Republican president taking orders from a Russian dictator. "Fashion student Lila Hekekia has deemed Ulla Ultimate's models and show in need of the second coming—Lila's own show—as promised by Ulla's past college sweetheart and Lila's current college squeeze, Associate Professor of Fashion Tyler Greenway. Ulla was as angry at sonny Cory's come-on to Shane and Julio, as Cory was miffed by the two models ultimately (*no pun intended*) rejecting him. Ulla's minion, Miles Jeffrey, has orders to marry off sonny Ultimate. Stage manager Hoss Packer and seamster Johnny Riley were fed up with Shane and Julio's moves on Hoss and jabs at Johnny."

Martin replied like a gambling addict missing a chip, "What about the model who eats all the time?"

"That's Cosmo Capra. He was fed up (*no pun intended*) with Shane and Julio calling him on it." I added, "Then there's the ghost."

Four heads cocked in my direction and Shayla gasped.

I explained, "When I was alone in the fashion theatre, I saw the figure of a beautiful blonde woman in white satin."

Ruben asked, "How do you know she was a ghost?"

"I don't." I slid to the edge of my seat. "I guess she could be a fashion student practicing during spring break. All I know is she was mystifying, majestic, and magical." *Try saying that three times fast while applying lip moisturizer.* "If she were a man, I'd put her in Julio's place on the runway."

Taavi perked up. "Pop, since there's an empty spot in the show, and because I can change quickly, how about if I wear two outfits per set?"

"I'll remember your willingness to change quickly

when you sleep late for school in the morning."

"Come on, Pop. My fans will want to see me in more than one outfit per category."

"Then your fans can watch you in your room when you change clothes endlessly before a date with Tia."

Martin was just about to doze off until he heard that. "Tell me, Taavi, are things heating up with you and the little seamstress?"

Taavi winked at him. "Who says puberty isn't fun?"

Martin grinned. "You and your Uncle Martin will need some alone time to…share all of your fascinating stories about Tia."

"Shouldn't that be *Auntie* Martin—or Auntie Mame?" Ruben asked with a sneer.

Shayla cackled wildly. "Good one, Ruben."

Martin sniffed. "Shayla, don't your wife and young daughter need you at home?"

"This is way more fun," she replied.

"Well, you won't be laughing when the audience cheers for *me* in the show."

I hiccupped. "You? In the show?"

Martin swallowed the last of his drink and then placed the cup and saucer on top of his desk. "As I reminded Ruben the other day, I was once a male model in magazines. However, I always regretted not having my time down the runway. While Julio's passing was tragic, it may be the pot at the end of my runway rainbow."

"Accent on rainbow," Ruben added.

Shayla appeared at the doorway in a burgundy business suit. Her dark eyes seemed to have tripled in size. "Martin, are you actually saying that you want to be a model in the fashion show?"

"I am."

Ruben interceded. "Wearing what, Martin? A senior diaper?"

Shayla pressed a dark stray hair into the bun at the

back of her neck. "And how will you make it all the way down the runway, Martin? Wouldn't a walker slow down the show? Not to mention the chairlift for the stairs!"

"Don't worry, Shayla, it's not happening."

Martin, hearing his husband's words, rose like a malaria victim's temperature. "How can you deny me my one unfulfilled dream?"

"Because your dream would be the *Ultimate* nightmare." Ruben stood next to his husband. "As co-producer, I must put my foot down."

"On my heart!" Martin sobbed into a lavender handkerchief.

Shayla flew to Martin's other side. "The models in the show are a quarter of your age, Martin."

"And they have a quarter of my know-how!" Martin strode up and down his office. "There's nothing more exhilarating than having all eyes upon you on the runway."

"All eyes will be on you all right." Shayla snickered.

Martin replied, "Shayla, have you ever done any modeling?"

"No. Acting in your cockamamie plays and role-plays to catch murderers is enough for me." She pointed to herself. "And do I look like a model?"

Martin said, "Possibly. Full-figure gals are in nowadays."

"And unfortunately for you, stick-figure crazy old men are out!"

Ruben held back Shayla. "Hopefully he's having a senior moment."

Martin seethed. "Shayla, please tell my husband, what's his name, he can't keep me chained to my desk. My career as a model must come first!"

Ruben smirked. "Forgetting your spouse's name is a sign of dementia, Martin."

Martin replied, "You know me: out of sight, out of

mind."

"Yes, Martin, 'out of sight and out of mind' describes you perfectly."

Taavi giggled as if watching a comedy routine. Noah shushed him.

Ruben seized the opportunity. "Even the boy realizes how ridiculous you are behaving, Martin."

I took pity on my best friend. Standing across from him, I said, "Martin may be on to something."

"Or *on* something," Ruben replied.

I explained, "The fashion show is highlighting men's fashion. We have a young teenager, college students, and a nearly middle-aged man in the show. Why not add someone of advanced age?"

Shayla's dark face turned pale. "Martin is beyond advanced, Nicky. He's prehistoric!"

Noah came to my side and to my rescue. "Nicky's right. Everyone wears clothes. I think it will make the show more realistic to have men of all ages represented."

Martin embraced us. "Thank you, Nicky and Noah. It's nice to know my mentees are on my side. I'll ask that clumsy freshman fashion student, Johnny Riley, to fit me in Julio's wardrobe."

Hope you don't mind blood on it.

Martin collapsed into the chair behind his cherry desk. "Now, since *that's* settled, and Manuello is otherwise engaged, shouldn't we plan our first role-play to catch the murderer?"

Shayla rubbed her hands together. "Count me in! There's nothing I like better than watching you guys make fools of yourselves."

Taavi joined the rest of us at Martin's desk. "I'm in too, Pop."

"Who's the first victim?" Ruben asked, licking his lips.

"The suspect we know the least about." I put my arms arounds them. "Listen up, everyone. Here's the plan."

After I filled in my little troupe, Martin and Ruben went home to practice for Martin's runway premiere. Noah, Taavi, Shayla, and I had dinner in the college cafeteria as we rehearsed our roles. Then Noah led us to the costume and makeup areas back in the Theatre Department building, where my talented spouse worked his magic on the three of us.

Early that evening, Taavi, Shayla, and I stood in the front lobby of the fashion building's theatre. I gazed into the mirror on the pink wall and couldn't hold back my laughter. A long bleach blond wig led down to my gold jumpsuit, which was opened to the navel, leading down to an enormous crotch—thanks to my well-endowed status and a gym sock for good measure. My exposed skin peeled from a fake orange tan. Next to me, Taavi stood in white undies with a blond wig and dark sunglasses. On my other side, Shayla was squeezed into a white spandex blouse and slacks with a carrot red wig on her head. She looked like a bowl of vanilla and chocolate ice cream with a cherry on top.

Cosmo Capra entered the lobby in a Prussian blue suit—a bit tight at the middle. He scanned the otherwise empty lobby and then made his way over to us. "Excuse me, Professor Abbondanza phoned me about an appointment here this evening."

I replied in a thick Italian accent (that sounded like a Martian speaking French with a Dutch accent). "You are Cosmo Capra, eh?"

"Yes. Professor Abbondanza didn't give me *your* name?"

I gasped and placed my hand on my bare chest. My gold rings got caught in the hair. "You don't know me!"

"I'm afraid not. I've been pretty busy with my schoolwork."

I fumed. "You must be studying under a rock, eh! Don't you see the covers of cheap romance paperbacks?

Watch infomercials on television? See straight porn after midnight on your computer?"

"I'm sorry."

"Everyone has heard of Fey Bene, the most famous male model of all time!" I squeezed my pecs and flicked back my blond hair.

Cosmo fudged. "Right. I think I've heard about you."

"Everyone has heard about Fey Bene, no?" I pointed to Shayla. "And of course you recognize the most famous female ex-model in the world, Brooke Shills."

Shayla placed a hand on her abundant hip and offered a wide smile.

I explained, "After all those failed television shows, she put on a bit of weight, capisci?"

Cosmo nodded. "I'm currently a model in the Ultimate Fashion Show here on campus. I've put on a bit of weight too."

"Ultimate Fashion, feh!" Shayla got a bit too excited and nearly knocked off her wig. After cagily shouting, "Look outside at the beautiful sunset," she quickly repaired the damage then said, "My department store clothing line is much more chic than those black leather monstrosities from Ulla." She patted her hips. "And my clothes are more practical." She beckoned him closer with an index finger. "You ever go to the mall?"

Cosmo nodded. "To the food emporium."

"The women you see there, do they look like models?"

He shook his head, and black hair flew in all directions.

"Of course not. They look like *me*. So *my* clothes win!" Shayla laughed heartily.

I completed the introductions. "And of course you recognize this young fellow in his black shades and tighty whities."

Cosmo squinted at him.

Taavi gyrated his body, spun in the air, and ended on the floor in a split. "Macky Mac Mack."

Try saying that three times fast while kissing someone.

When Cosmo seemed confused, Taavi struck a masculine pose. "I'm a young rock star turned model and soon-to-be a movie star, dude. You can catch me on cool billboards all over the city, bro."

Cosmo scratched at his head. "Which city?"

I interjected, "*Every* city that values culture and the arts, si?"

"It's nice to meet you all." Cosmo shuffled from one dress shoe to the other. "But I'm not sure why Professor Abbondanza asked me here. He sounded rushed on the phone."

Pointing to a pink and silver loveseat near the window, I announced, "Please step into my office."

Cosmo cocked his head. "I thought this was the front lobby of the fashion theatre."

"It is! Currently on loan to me as my office, amico."

Once the three of us were seated on the loveseat with Cosmo perched on a matching easy chair across from us, I explained, "Mr. Capra, my business associate, the incredibly gifted and talented, and not to mention very handsome and bright, Professor Abbondanza, said good things to me—about you. Bene. Bene. And I trust Professor Abbondanza's sound judgment implicitly, paesano."

Cosmo slid to the edge of his seat. "What did Professor Abbondanza say about me?"

"That you are loaded with…untapped talent, bursting at the seams…with possibilities, stuffed…with potential, eh?"

Cosmo relaxed. "That was very nice of him."

"Not nice!" I squeezed his round knee. "It is true. I can tell." Glancing at the shirt button about to pop at his middle, I added, "In our brief time together so far, you have oozed…future success, no?"

Taavi took over. "But as I learned when I finally got my big break at five years old: to succeed, you need the seed."

"The seed?"

I explained to Cosmo, "If you want to be a successful model, you need help from the best — us."

"Or help from a pushy mother." Shayla rested her palms on her stomach.

Cosmo ran a hand through his hair. "You mean, you three people are offering to help me become a professional model?"

"You're catching on now, dude." Taavi slapped him a high five.

"And you won't even have to take off all your clothes, like I did as a kid." Shayla scratched at her bottom.

Cosmo seemed quite touched. "That's really generous of you — all. I don't know what to say."

"Say you'll work with us, amico."

Cosmo offered me a smile bigger than the campaign war chest of a conservative politician owned by a large corporation. "I will! Thank you. Where do we start?"

I spread my legs. "At the core, eh?"

"Excuse me?"

Shayla explained, "Before we can advise you on the business, we need to know more about *you*."

"Like what makes you cooler than the rest, dude?" Taavi added.

A crease appeared across Cosmo's forehead. "Well, I'm getting a college degree."

Shayla giggled. "I got one of those. Didn't help me much. I still had to take off my clothes to get jobs. What else?"

Cosmo offered, "Well, I'm always on time."

"We aren't helping you get a job as an efficiency expert, baby." Taavi shook his head. "What makes you hot, in the now, set apart from the rest, my man?"

Cosmo glanced down at his stomach. "I weigh a bit more than most male models."

I asked, "Why is that?"

"Because I eat pretty much nonstop."

"You have a tapeworm, baby?" Taavi asked.

Cosmo shook his head. "It's because of my sister."

"She's a good cook like my mother?" Shayla asked.

"No." Cosmo smiled affectionately. "But she was a good person. Warm and caring." He added as if just realizing it, "I think she was my only friend."

Taavi folded his arms over his chest. "*Was*, dude?"

Cosmo looked down at the pink and silver rug. "She passed away last year."

Poor kid. "What happened?"

His face lit up like a sconce. "Cynthia was always a gullible kid. Three years younger than me, she looked to her older brother for direction. And I gave it freely — all the time." Tears filled his sad eyes. "Except once."

"Care to tell us about it, paesano?"

Cosmo took in a deep breath. "There was no girl prettier than Cynthia. I know that sounds a bit kinky coming from her brother, but it's true. Her hair was like soft silk. Her eyes deeper than the ocean. And her skin like buttermilk. But it wasn't only her looks. Cynthia had a way of making you want to shield her from the world and take care of her. We'd sit up nights in my room sharing our hopes and desires and planning our futures. Cynthia was top in her class. I wasn't. She was gorgeous and talented. I wasn't that either. But we both had the same dream: to become models. I know that's a strange dream for a straight guy."

He's straight?

"But for whatever reason anybody wants anything, that's what I wanted. And so did Cynthia. With Cynthia's terrific looks and charisma, a modeling agent discovered her freshman year of high school. I was so happy for her." Cosmo was lost in his memories. "Cynthia was the best runway model I've ever seen. You should have heard the crowds cheer. And her pictures on magazine covers doubled their sales. Her agent talked about television possibilities—which excited Cynthia to no end. It also caused her to eat more. Cynthia was always a nervous eater. It runs in our family. So, when she gained some weight, her agent issued a warning: stop eating or stop being a model." Cosmo stared at us with puppy dog eyes. "Who said every model has to be emaciated and starving?" He answered his own question. "Everybody in the industry." His shoulders slumped. "So Cynthia starved herself until she lost the weight. But she didn't stop there. Due to her agent's constant warnings about eating too much, Cynthia actually believed she was overweight. So she ate less, and less, and finally she didn't eat at all." The tears streamed down his cheeks. "Why didn't I insist that she eat something? Why didn't I force the food down her throat?"

"It might not have made a difference. Your sister had a disease—anorexia nervosa. It's a compulsive disorder." Shayla glanced down at her stomach. "Not all models suffer from it, but many do."

Cosmo nodded. "That's what her doctor said. She saw a psychiatrist three times a week, but it didn't help. And when the modeling work dried up because Cynthia was too thin, she decided the jobs were cut off because she was too fat. So she started inducing her own vomit. By that time, I finally stepped in and demanded that she begin eating. But it was too late. She died a week later." He wept openly.

I leaned forward and rested my hand on his shoulder. "I'm so sorry."

He nodded, wiping his face with the sleeve of his jacket. "I wish every model, every person, would understand how dangerous it is to go on a severe diet. Everyone everywhere should realize the dangers of starving themselves in a senseless pursuit of having the perfect body. People on magazine covers have touch-up artists. Nobody can look like that. And who wants to anyway?" He grimaced. "And those who mock others' bodies and call people 'fat' should be ashamed of themselves. They're contributing to the self-loathing and insecurity of anyone with a negative body image. And who are these people to judge anyway? Who elected them to be the deciders of which bodies are acceptable and which aren't? How dare they mock someone for the simple act of eating?" He pounded his fist into the palm of his hand. "Anyone who treats another person like that is a parasite who doesn't deserve to live!"

After offering my condolences, I took a chance. "Is anyone in your current show mocking *your* weight?"

Cosmo nodded. "Yeah, Shane Buff and Julio Bonero."

"I'll bet they angered you."

Cosmo nodded again.

"So you killed them!"

Cosmo flinched. "No! I didn't kill anybody." Tears filled his eyes. "I kept my anger inside and ate."

The three of us gave Cosmo some (*off the cuff*) advise on modeling. He thanked us profusely and then went on his way.

While Taavi and Shayla changed their clothes back in the theatre building, I entered the fashion theatre house through the lobby door. Again, the theatre was darkened (*the way I like it*). I assumed Manuello, his lackeys, and the targets of his interrogations had all gone home. Glancing around the house, I spotted something white. Shifting my focus to the stage, I noticed the ghost model glide across the runway, the blonde hair and white satin gown flowing behind her. Surprisingly, I felt happy to see her and not fearful in any way. Since I was close to the lip of the runway, I called out, "Who are you?"

She stood frozen.

"Please, tell me why you are here."

She gasped and disappeared backstage.

Realizing the others would be waiting for me, I hurried back to the theatre building, changed out of my costume — bidding Fay Bene farewell, and Noah drove Taavi and me home at the speed of lightning.

After heading upstairs and changing into our T-shirts and boxers, the three of us did our nightly ritual of tucking Taavi into bed. Like a celebrity stalking a potential fan, Taavi asked us, "How did I do with my role-play?"

I kissed his forehead. "You were wonderful. Almost as convincing as me."

"Can I have some mustard with that ham sandwich?"

Taavi and I laughed at Noah's joke.

Noah lifted the sheet over Taavi's neck. "Taavi, you know that murder is serious business."

"Sure, Dad. That's why I love it — just as much as I love show business." Taavi reached for his phone on the night table.

I said, "It's bedtime."

"But I have to text Tia."

Noah smiled. "I know you like Tia, but do you think the constant communication with her is necessary?"

"It's what she wants, Dad."

"And you?"

"I want what Tia wants, Pop."

Spoken like a straight man. "Get some sleep. Tomorrow we're rehearsing the mid-show number." I rose and shut the light with Noah behind me.

"I'll be ready." Taavi added in the dark, "And I'll keep an eye out for anything suspicious."

The light of his phone beamed under the sheet as we left his room and shut the door behind us.

The moment Noah and I were under our silk sheet and resting in each other's welcoming arms, I filled him in on our role-play.

My sweet Noah said, "What a heartbreaking story about Cosmo's sister."

"It explains a lot about Cosmo's culinary habits. And why he told Taavi to eat whatever he wants at rehearsals."

"More importantly, it explains Cosmo's anger at Shane and Julio for mocking his weight."

I cuddled Noah further into my chest and enjoyed his strawberry scent. "Though Cosmo denied it, he has a clear motive for murder."

Noah tented the sheet.

"Somebody's excited."

He giggled. "Hearing you talk like a detective stimulates me."

I kissed his shoulder. "Is that so, Dr. Watson?"

Reaching under the sheet, Noah replied, "That's definitely so, Mr. Holmes."

I hurried into the bathroom for my new cream, leapt back into bed, slathered it all over our bodies, and Sherlock and John had a sexy encounter.

I fell asleep soon afterward with dreams of Cosmo carving a turkey and then stabbing Shane and Julio with the knife. In my last dream, the model in white lifted Shane and Julio from the ground and flew them to Model Heaven.

I woke late the next morning. Once I had showered and put on my new body cream, I ate breakfast in the nook with my guys (poached egg and roasted tomato smothered in zamorano cheese on oatbread) and downed my vitamins with a pear avocado parsley smoothie. Then Noah sped us to campus faster than an evangelical clerk refusing a gay couple a marriage license. The sky was bluer than a KKK member meeting a minority, as the three of us walked across the campus, admiring the just budding flowers at the base of the white Edwardian buildings. The turquoise lake and stoic mountains in the distance offered false shielding from the dangers that lie ahead of us as we approached the fashion building.

We walked around the building, through the alley, and into the dressing room, noticing the yellow tapes were all gone. Martin was already there, gazing at himself in a floor-length mirror. Posing in a long black leather one-piece swimsuit, Martin said to Ruben standing next to him, "I feel so incredibly bold."

Ruben replied, "And you look so incredibly old."

As Taavi and Noah changed into their black leather trunks and Speedos respectively, I noticed Cory Ultimate, in a black leather thong, huddled in a corner with his mother's assistant, Miles Jeffrey.

Cory smirked at the twenty-three-year-old wearing a conservative pinstriped blue suit. "How's the crusade going to get me married off, Miles?"

Miles clicked on a file in his laptop. "I interviewed Cosmo Capra, twenty, fashion major."

"Not interested."

"That's what he said."

"I meant *I'm* not interested in *him*."

"The feeling's mutual."

Cosmo's affections seem to be wrapped around his heterosexuality and his candy bars.

Miles closed the file. "Three strikes."

"And I'm *out*." Cory smiled and spread his arms like a chorus boy.

"I won't give up."

"Mother would have it no other way." Cory rubbed his hands together. "In the meanwhile, I want to say 'humplo' to our hunky stage manager. Dark chocolate is so good for me, and it's quite tasty going down."

Miles sighed. "Don't you ever get tired of that?"

Cory faced him. "Tired of what?"

"The childish act you put on for your mother. Throwing yourself at guys who aren't right for you, and who aren't interested in you."

"Did my mother tell you to ask me that?"

"No." Miles added, "I call things as I see them."

"And what exactly do you see?"

Miles' eyes bore into his. "I see a young man with incredible potential throwing his body and his life away in an attempt to win his mother's love, which he already has, but he is too self-absorbed to realize it. So instead of trying to make a success of himself, he blames his mother for his failures, which if he doesn't change his ways will compound as he gets older."

Cory's nostrils flared. "Let me return the 'favor' and call a few things as I see them, Miles. Being Ulla Ultimate's assistant gives you a sense of self-worth—without you having to make your own way in the world. So, you hide behind my mother's black leather apron because you lost your own mother. Here's a news flash for you, Miles. Your mother's dead, and you can't have mine! Your father's dead too. And you can't have my father either. Whoever he is."

Miles handed Cory his laptop. "Find your own husband, Cory. Then get married and move far away." He took off.

Cory followed him. "Wait! Miles!"

I crossed over to the sewing room, where Tia was working busily at her machine. She looked adorable in a pink blouse and denim shorts with her dark hair in a ponytail. "Oh."

"Something wrong, Tia?"

"Hi, Mr. Abbondanza. I thought you might be Taavi."

"Sorry to disappoint you."

"It's cool." She checked her phone. "Taavi just texted he'll be right over." She continued repairing the hem of a black leather coat.

"Tia, I hope you're not too upset about the murders. To be honest, I had assumed your parents wouldn't let you continue here."

She nodded. "They were upset about it. But I told them how much I wanted to be with Taavi, and how you and Mr. Oliver are always nearby. They finally agreed to let me come back."

"I'm glad they did. So is Taavi."

She smiled. "We're a perfect couple. Just like my parents."

And Noah and I are gay chopped liver? "Well, have a good day, Tia."

"You too, Mr. Abbondanza."

I moved on to Johnny Riley at his machine.

"Ow!"

"Johnny, are you all right?"

He applied a bandage to his elbow. "My fault. I accidentally leaned into a pin cushion."

Hoss Packer arrived through the outside door, his muscles sculpted inside a coral T-shirt and jeans. "Johnny, can I talk to you?"

Johnny replied, "I have a lot of work to do."

"Please? Just for a minute?"

Johnny stood and banged into his sewing machine. "Ouch!" Holding his knee, he hobbled over toward the door.

I pretended to check my messages on my phone while I listened.

Hoss cleared his throat, a bit out of breath. "I just came from the gym."

"I'm guessing you go there a lot," Johnny replied.

"Yeah."

"I went once but never again."

"How come?"

"I tried to use the pull-down bar and hung myself by mistake. It took two personal trainers and an EMT to rescue me."

Hoss smiled. "We should go to the gym together

sometime."

"I don't think that's a good idea. I'd cramp your style."

"Then let's get some dinner after rehearsal today?"

Johnny held his stomach. "I probably shouldn't eat anything. I fell on a scissors and I think I'm bleeding internally."

Hoss laughed. "I don't think you're bleeding internally."

"Hopefully not."

"But I do think you've been avoiding me. And I think I know why."

Johnny turned away. "It's because I'm totally weird."

"Yeah, but I'm kind of weird too."

Johnny did a double take. "You're not weird at all. You're perfect."

Hoss guffawed. "I'm far from perfect. Just ask my roommate at the dorm. I'm messy, and I talk in my sleep. And I always forget to do my laundry, so I have to wear my clothes inside out."

Johnny smiled. "I do those things too."

"See? We have a lot in common."

"Except my roommate moved out the first week of classes. He said he'd rather sleep in a tent infested with snakes than room with me. Back home in Washington, my parents built an extension on our house for me, and then they locked the door on the other side."

"How about this? Back home in Ohio, my mom had to tutor me every night, so I could pass high school algebra."

"Is your mom a math teacher?"

Hoss nodded. "Which made it all the more embarrassing."

"How about your dad?"

"He left when I was three."

"Why? Did he have problems with algebra too?"

Hoss roared with laughter. "You crack me up, Johnny."

"I crack myself up too." He showed Hoss his bandaged

head. "I banged my head on the broom while I was sweeping the shop floor."

"Johnny, have you ever considered that sewing isn't for you?"

He nodded. "But I love the fashion world, and it's the only thing I can do."

"How about designing?"

"I kept stabbing myself with the drafting pens, and the computer programs made me dizzy and I fainted." Johnny sighed. "I'd love to be a model." Pointing to the navy-blue T-shirt and jeans hanging off his body like wilted plants, he added, "But that's clearly not in my future."

"I disagree with you there."

Johnny quickly changed the subject. "Why do you want to be a stage manager?"

"Because I like managing things."

"It seems that a lot of guys around here would like you to manage *them.*"

"I don't pay attention to that."

"Even the guys who were killed?"

That caught my attention.

"I don't want to sound callous, but I've always believed life is about the living." Hoss rested a large hand on Johnny's quivering cheek. "Johnny, I really like you, and I think you like me too."

"Who wouldn't like someone as wonderful as you?"

"And I'd really like to spend some time with you."

"You don't have to say that because of what happened."

Hoss placed a hand on his shoulder. "We need to talk about that."

"I can't. I'm sorry." Johnny hurried off.

I left the sewing room and entered the theatre down the runway. I called everyone into the house for an audience to my dramatic and heartbreaking speech in honor of Julio Bonero. Since my vivid performance was met with sidebar whispering and texting (*like my class lectures*), I called out for "places" to resume the rehearsal where we had left off.

The back door of the theatre opened, and Associate Professor of Fashion Tyler Greenway barreled inside with his mass contained in a vermillion sweater and black slacks. Clearly a bit tipsy, he swayed over to Ulla Ultimate at her aisle seat toward the center of the theatre. Ulla, clad in a black leather sundress, choker, and long boots, glanced up at him like a top one-percenter being asked to pay taxes.

"Ulla, you have to help me!"

She rose and pulled back her bare shoulders. "That phrase brings back memories."

"Lila Hekekia, my student with the big...mouth is suing me for sexual harassment."

Ulla cringed. "Are you drunk, Tyler? Another familiar memory."

"Can you blame me? This could end my teaching career."

"Perhaps you should have thought about that *before* carrying on with your student. But, as I recall, you never did think about the results of your actions."

He placed an arm around her. "Ulla, please, you can make this all go away. You owe me this for stealing my designs back in college. Just give Lila a spot in your show."

She shrugged him away. "My designs are mine. And my show is mine. And that's final!"

Tyler's face soured. "You're the same cold, vicious bitch I remember, Ulla."

"And you're the same repugnant, selfish cretin I've tried to forget."

The back door opened again, and Lila entered in a skintight strawberry tube top and cranberry miniskirt. She wore more makeup than a silent movie star. "Here you are, Tyler. Well, what will it be? My own spring show as you promised me, or a sexual harassment charge followed by an accusation of religious discrimination?"

Tyler begged. "Please, Ulla! Help me!"

Ulla folded her arms over her chest. "Not this time, Tyler."

On that happy note, I called for "quiet," and "lights up."

At the rear of the theatre, Hoss punched endless keys on the computerized lighting board until the house lights finally went down and the stage lights came up. The models entered the runway in their bathing suits while singing a song about the "hard" life of a model: "A Model Puts Out." Having watched previous rehearsals choreographed by Noah, Martin was right in step with the hip-hop choreography, even surpassing the energy of the younger models. Taavi, of course, stole the show with his added swimming choreography and dive off the runway. As Cory danced, he glanced out at Miles in the audience, who instantly diverted his gaze. It suddenly occurred to me that Cosmo Capra was not on the stage. *As a matter of fact, I haven't seen Cosmo all day.* "Stop!"

Hoss turned off the music and brought up the house lights (*eventually*) as I leapt up the steps, and across the runway. Noah was behind me like a shadow. After searching the dressing room, we moved into the sewing room. Noah pointed to a shoe peeking out from behind the fabric cabinet. "Nicky!"

After we moved the cabinet from the wall, I peered down at Cosmo Capra's prostrate body, noticing his mouth had been sewn closed. *His lips are sealed.*

CHAPTER FIVE

While Manuello and his posse taped off the sewing room, and dusted, prodded, and bagged evidence, I went outside for some air. When I spotted a lit camera and microphone, I ran toward it, more excited than a televangelist after pledge week with a new mansion. Fashion student Lila Hekekia was being interviewed by a young female reporter. Like Lila, the reporter wore skintight clothing, heavy makeup, and gold jewelry. The journalist said to the camera, "I'm speaking with Lila Hekekia, a freshman fashion major at Treemeadow College. Lila, three male modeling students have been killed in the fashion building. Tell us what you know."

Lila flipped her dark braid behind her shoulder and batted her fake eyelashes at the camera. "The students were modeling in Visiting Professor Ulla Ultimate's spring fashion show." She grimaced. "I'm not surprised they came to a bad end."

The reporter looked hungrier than an abandoned animal in a shelter. "Why is that?"

Lila smacked her cherry lips. "The spring show was originally promised to *me* by my professor, Tyler Greenway, who seduced me."

"So Ulla Ultimate stole a seduced student's show?"

Try saying that three times fast while eating a slushie.

Lila nodded. "And she filled it with homosexual male models glorifying S&M."

The reporter noticed me — after I flung myself in front

of the camera. "Professor Abbondanza, you've solved many murder mysteries at Treemeadow College in the past."

"Yes, I have." I winked at the camera.

"And you are the director of the Ultimate Fashion Show."

"Which I predict will win numerous awards—mostly for me."

"You are also an extremely active homosexual."

"You flatter me. Noah and I are generally active only about twice a week."

The reporter grimaced. "And you live a deviant lifestyle with a minor."

"Taavi's texting is annoying, but 'deviant' is a bit harsh."

The reporter's voice seemed to get more strident by the syllable. "Can you possibly defend Professor Ultimate's show celebrating perversion?"

I raised my hand. "I defend perversion whenever I can."

Lila's fake nails clutched at my shoulder and she pushed me out of the camera frame. "The God Loves Only the Rich Organization is funding my sexual harassment suit against Professor Greenway, my religious discrimination case against Treemeadow College, and my upcoming family-friendly summer fashion show in place of the Ultimate disgrace."

The reporter aimed the microphone at my grateful face. "Nicky, what do you have to say to the decent people of faith everywhere who support Ms. Hekekia in her one-Christian-woman's battle against the powerful homosexual lobby?"

"I'd say Jesus was a single, poor radical travelling with twelve other single men, serving everyone and preaching acceptance for all. Sounds to me like Jesus's lobby was a lot like mine."

Lila shrieked and pointed. "Blasphemy! That's illegal discrimination against my religious beliefs!"

I smiled at her. "Our beliefs may not be that different, Lila. Heck, Jesus hid in a cave and rose a man from the dead. I think the savior and I have a lot in common."

"Fake news!" Lila turned to the camera. "This is the kind of twisted thinking that elevates poor people, foreigners, those who are sick, and homosexuals to think they are worthy of God's love. It also leads to depraved fashion shows like Professor Ultimate's."

I replied, "You know that isn't true, Lila."

"Yes it is. It's alternate news."

"Lila, my fashion show isn't so bad." I nudged her shoulder. "I'll bet Jesus really strutted his stuff in that white robe when he walked on water."

Lila's face turned blue. "This is the kind of degeneracy that leads to the three young men being murdered!"

The reporter chimed in. "Speaking of the murders, what can you tell us about the investigation, Nicky? Should the people of Treemeadow be afraid?"

"Yes, they should."

She signaled her camera operator to come in for a close-up on me.

Actually, I did the signaling. "They should fear that our show may sell out! So, citizens of Treemeadow, if you haven't already, purchase your tickets for Ulla Ultimate's wonderful spring fashion show!" I smiled. "Did I mention the show is directed by *me*?"

Noah appeared at my side. "And I, Associate Professor of Acting, Noah Oliver, am one of the models."

Martin was at my other side like a fast-growing weed. "As am I, Professor of Theatre Management and Theatre Department Head, Martin Anderson."

"I'm Ruben, Martin's husband. If you think your life is rough, imagine mine," he said over his husband's shoulder.

I felt something move between my legs. (*It's not what*

you're thinking.) Looking down, I saw Taavi spring forth like a beanstalk. "And I, Taavi Kapule Oliver Abbondanza, am the star model in the show."

Tia emerged next to him. "And I'm his girlfriend, seamstress, and future theatrical costume designer, Tia Tedesco."

She's one of the family.

The reporter seemed frustrated. "And the three murders in the fashion building?"

I took a step forward—and banged my chin on the microphone. "As I have done so many times in the past, I give the good people of Treemeadow my solemn oath that I, Nicky Abbondanza, PhD, will squeeze out the murderer like a liberal at a gun show, and once again restore regularity to Treemeadow!"

"With my help!" Noah, Martin, Ruben, Taavi, and Tia added in unison.

"Agh!" I felt a hand at the back of my blazer collar, and then I watched my shoes drag along the cobblestone. The next thing I knew, I was standing opposite Manuello in the lobby of the fashion theatre.

"How many times do I have to tell you not to speak to the press?"

"Is this a gay knock-knock joke for your new act, Manuello?" I straightened my blazer.

"So help me, Nicky."

"That's exactly what my family and I were trying to do out there, Manuello."

"My police officers are taking care of your motley crew."

I placed my hand over my heart. "Will you have them thrown in prison? Read them their last rites? Force them to donate to the Detective Benevolent Fund?"

"Relax, Nicky. My officers are taking them to wait with the others in the theatre."

I gasped. "Surely you don't suspect my family and

friends of murder?"

"No, but I need to talk to you alone before I interview the real suspects."

"Well it's nice to hear you finally admit you need me."

"I didn't say I need you. I said I need to talk to you."

"You don't have to play semantics with me, Manuello." I blew him a kiss. "I know you're crazy about me."

"Crazy just about sums it up."

I sat on the pink chaise and patted the seat next to me. "Let's talk about my case."

He sighed, plopped down, and removed the pad and pen from his wrinkled jacket pocket. "What do you have for me, Nicky?"

"Far too much for you to handle."

"I meant about Cosmo Capra's murder."

"*I* found the body."

"Of course."

"And this fashion theatre is currently loaded with people who wanted Cosmo dead."

"I'm listening."

I started to rise.

He pushed me back down. "Can we do this without the Sherlock Holmes pacing routine?"

"I thought that turned you on."

"To be honest, I've been suffering from vertigo lately."

"Vertigo?"

"It means dizziness."

"I know what vertigo means, Manuello. What I don't understand is why you wouldn't tell *me*, your trusted friend and unrequited love of your life, that you probably have a serious neurological disorder, brain tumor, or stroke!"

Manuello did a doubletake. "Is vertigo a symptom of those things?"

"In many cases."

Sweat beads formed on his olive-colored forehead. "I thought it might be from overwork."

"Hardly."

"Or from stress, low blood pressure, diabetes, or the start of a thyroid condition."

"Which can all kill you if left untreated."

"Really?"

"Most definitely. I'm worried about you, Manuello. I think you should go to the emergency room immediately and leave me to work on my case."

He groaned. "I see what you're doing, Nicky."

"What am I doing?"

"Trying to get rid of me so you can play detective."

I gasped. "Well, that's the thanks I get for being concerned about you."

"Don't be concerned about me. Just tell me about the suspects."

"Though I am a brilliant actor, I can't pretend that I don't worry about you. Especially now that the room is spinning around you out of control, and you can't even stand up without falling prostrate to the floor."

"Nicky, nothing is spinning out of control except my temper. So, unless you want me to spin you over that bar —"

I raised a finger. "Please, Manuello, no sexual fantasies about me."

"Tell me about the suspects or I'll take that finger and —!"

"Will your obsession with my body ever end?"

"Nicky!"

I blurted out quickly, "Cosmo Capra ate more than a dieter after weigh-in. Ulla Ultimate wanted Cosmo out of her show and in a fat farm. When Ulla's lackey, Miles Jeffrey, asked Cosmo about Ulla's son Cory, our latest victim rejected the idea of dating Cory, dubiously claiming his heterosexuality."

"Who dubiously claimed to be heterosexual?"

"Cosmo. And *you* of course." I clapped my hands together. "Ah, is that another joke for your gay stand-up act?"

"Keep going."

"I'm not a comedy writer, Manuello. I can't supply material for your act."

"I meant with the suspects and motives!"

"Fashion student slash evangelical Lila Hekekia took one look at Cosmo and spouted that gluttony is a sin. Her professor, Tyler Greenway, mentioned problems with Cosmo refusing to stop eating in class. Fashion student Johnny Riley's bandaged back went up when Cosmo asked hunky stage manager Hoss Packer about his diet."

"Who's diet?"

"Hoss's of course. But Johnny mistook Cosmo's interest in food."

"With what?"

"Interest in Hoss. Manuello, please try to keep up."

He threw his pen in the air. "These cases are like jigsaw puzzles."

I smiled. "And aren't you happy to have me to put all the pieces in place for you?"

He stood. "Here's a piece for you, Nicky. The governor and mayor are leaning on me."

"Are you sure it isn't your vertigo?"

"So the fashion show is off until the murderer is apprehended."

I rose, angrier than a maligned Democrat on conservative news. "You know I can't catch the murderer if we don't have a show. I need to eavesdrop on the suspects."

"*I* know that, but the governor and the mayor don't."

"Well, tell them!"

He rested his head in his hands. "All right, Nicky. But until I do, your rehearsals are over. Now get out of here so

I can interview the suspects."

With Manuello out of my hair, I went back into the theatre house, sat behind Ulla Ultimate, pretended to review my notes — and listened.

"Lila is insane if she thinks I would give up my show," Ulla said.

Standing, or rather swaying, in the aisle next to her, Tyler Greenway said, "Lila's a determined young woman. Just like you were in college."

Ulla's eyes turned into violet slits. "Lila Hekekia and I have nothing in common. Except being foolish enough to become involved with you."

Tyler glared at her. "The best decision I ever made was leaving you after graduation."

"I couldn't agree more. So why not recreate that moment?"

He stormed off.

Ulla wiped a tear from her cheek and then turned to Miles Jeffrey, sitting on her other side. "With Cosmo deceased, I need you to fill in for him in the fashion show."

Miles' square jaw dropped to his thick neck. "I'm not a model!"

"Neither was Cosmo." Ulla adjusted a strand of her platinum wig. "You're an attractive young man. And you've attended every rehearsal. Simply walk down the runway in Cosmo's wardrobe and do his moves — without popping out of your clothes the way he did."

"I can't do that."

She glared at him. "Yes, you can Miles. Or you're out of a job."

Miles clammed up. "But I don't remember what Cosmo wore."

"Cory!" Ulla waved to her son who was standing over Hoss in the lighting booth.

When Cory arrived at her summons, she said, "Take Miles to the dressing room and show him Cosmo's outfits for the show."

"I can find the clothes myself." Miles brushed past them and disappeared up the runway to backstage with Cory following him.

Not wanting to miss a trick (*not literally*), I took off on their trail.

When I arrived at the dressing room doorway, I leaned back and watched.

Cory was handing Miles his laptop. "You left this with me."

Miles rested it on a makeup table. "I'll add my new notes later."

"I thought you stopped interviewing guys about marrying me."

Miles rubbed his long nose. "It was an idle threat. I need this job."

Cory sat at a makeup table. "What's the latest verdict?"

Miles took the seat next to him. "I talked to Hoss Packer. He wasn't interested in you either."

"So he told me."

"I also interviewed Johnny Riley."

"I'm not interested in him."

"You two have that in common."

"I told you nobody wants to settle down with me." Cory looked like a lost boy at a carnival. "I don't blame them."

Poor guy.

Miles cocked his head. "What do you mean?"

"I was awake all last night."

Miles smirked. "I'm not surprised."

"Alone. Thinking about what you said to me. And I realized something."

"That you hate my guts?"

"No, well, maybe a little."

Miles smiled. "What did you realize?"

"I've been throwing myself at guys who don't want

me."

"Didn't you know that already?"

Cory nodded. "And I want those guys even less than they want me." He moved a mop of brown hair off his forehead. "Somehow you saw right through my antics to get back at my mother."

"Or to get her attention."

Cory sighed. "Miles, you were right. I'm a total mess." Tears filled his big brown eyes. "And I shouldn't have blamed you for speaking the truth. I know I came down hard on you, but I want you know, I think you're a nice guy who's just trying to do his job, which is totally impossible because nobody would be warped enough to marry me."

Miles wiped a tear off Cory's cheek. "Underneath all your anger at your mom, I think you're a nice guy too."

They stared into each other's eyes.

Cory seemed to remember. "Are you going to model in the show?"

Miles answered like a death row inmate, "It seems that way."

"Then I should show you Cosmo's outfits."

Miles extended an arm. "Show away."

Cory led Miles to a clothing rack. "The next section of the show is for kink."

Miles groaned.

"Put this on." Cory handed Miles black leather short shorts, boots, chains, and a cap.

"I must really want this job." Miles begrudgingly took the clothes and disappeared behind a screen. A minute later, he appeared.

Cory staggered backwards and whistled. "Miles! Where have you been hiding that incredible body?"

Miles shrugged. "Inside my suit, I guess."

"You're a real muscle stud!"

Miles glanced at Cory, still in his leather costume from

the rehearsal. "You're not so bad yourself, kid." He smirked. "Do you feel as ridiculous as I do?"

"I feel totally ridiculous, but not about wearing these clothes. About my whole life."

"Maybe it's time to settle down."

"Says the man wearing chains across his bare chest."

They shared a laugh.

I headed back into the theatre. From the runway, I looked out at the clusters of people who had not yet been called into the lobby for questioning by Manuello. Spotting Taavi and Tia talking to Lila Hekekia, I hightailed it over to the aisle at the third row.

Lila gushed. "Professor Abbondanza, you have an absolutely adorable son!"

"We agree on something, Lila."

"And he's Hawaiian, like me!"

Taavi offered her the hang loose sign.

Lila pinched his cheek. "Hurry and grow up so we can get married." She laughed, and her no doubt surgically-altered bosoms hardly moved. Then she whispered in my ear, "I'm so glad your son didn't follow in your footsteps and become a homosexual."

I grimaced. "I must have forgotten to give him the manual for Christmas."

"Thank goodness!" Lila patted Tia's head. "And he has this cute little child as his girlfriend. I'm jealous."

"Thank you." Tia held Taavi's hand (*no doubt worn out from texting*).

Lila played with her gold bracelets. "But that doesn't mean I approve of your lifestyle, Professor, or that I'm giving up my lawsuit. I won't back down."

Until you have your own fashion show.

Taavi tapped my elbow. "Pop, can I talk to you?"

"Sure. Please excuse us." I led Taavi to the rear of the theatre. "What is it?"

"I've been spying on everyone—for the case. And I

overheard Lila talking on her phone."

"Was she speaking with the almighty himself?"

"It sounded like she was making some kind of deal."

I was intrigued. "What kind of deal?"

"I don't know."

"What did she say?"

He replied sotto voce, "Lila said, 'I'll do water sports, a full Nelson, a pig roast, and a three-eyed turtle at the money shot for five grand.'"

Holy porn star, Batman. "Taavi, do you know what those words mean?"

He shook his head.

"Good. I'll take it from here."

Taavi held my arm. "Did I do some good investigating, Pop?"

I mussed his hair. "You sure did."

Elated, Taavi texted Tia as he walked back over to her.

Reaching for my phone, I searched a number of porn web sites (*straight ones for a change*) until I came to a picture of a porn star who resembled Lila: Kona Lingus the star of *Cherry Seed*. I marched over to her, phone in hand. "Lila, can I have a word?"

In the midst of spouting her religious beliefs to Taavi and Tia, Lila said, "I'm busy right now, Professor."

"Yes, it seems you've been very busy, Kona Lingus."

"Excuse me, children." Lila hurried to the back of the theatre, where the screen of my phone and I greeted her.

"Hypocrite, anyone?"

"I am not a hypocrite, Professor."

"Then what do you call a porn star who claims her religious freedom is being violated by a fashion show?"

"A good Christian one…like Mary Magdalen."

"Care to explain that one to a liberal Christian who isn't *that* liberal?"

Lila rested against the wall of the theatre. "All right, Professor. I'll explain. I'm a porn star for Jesus—to raise money for the campaigns of family-friendly politicians and judges who promise to stand firm against the rights of homosexuals and women. She sighed. "Please keep this between us."

I burst out laughing. "You're all over the internet!"

"But decent people don't look at those sites."

My head was reeling. "Lila, your so called 'religious freedom' case is busted after this. Your sexual harassment case may be as well."

"That's religious discrimination!"

"I'll tell you what's religious discrimination: you and your bigoted, two-faced, corrupt politicians and judges who would only love your neighbor as yourselves if the neighbor were white, straight, male, rich, greedy, and as arrogant as you!"

She seethed with rage. "You'll eat those words when I sue you, and the Republican-appointed evangelical judge awards me millions of dollars in damages. Like the Christians brought to the lions, I'll fight until I win big bucks and become famous on conservative news shows!" Lila stormed into the lobby.

Republican Jesus is one scary guy. Since Manuello wouldn't allow us to continue rehearsing, I asked Noah and Taavi to change out of their wardrobes. Then my husband drove us home faster than a Republican president waving a rainbow flag during the election and then removing all LGBT rights after inauguration.

After a quick snack in the kitchen, we spruced up the house, and then began preparations for our dinner party. Taavi headed upstairs to Skype with Tia about his wardrobe for the evening. I stood at the antique hutch in the dining room and passed Noah cream-colored satin napkins, silver, crystal glassware, and bone china. Noah placed them on our long maple table around the silver candleholders and flower centerpiece. "I hope Taavi and Tia aren't too traumatized by the latest murder."

I guffawed. "Hardly! Taavi is salivating to take over my case, and Tia seems to be going along happily for the ride."

"True. I saw her reading an Agatha Christie novel in the fashion theatre."

"No doubt while she texted Taavi."

Noah held a blue-and-white patterned plate. "Do you think Taavi and Tia are getting too serious too early?"

I shrugged. "In some ways thirteen is a lot older than it was decades ago."

"In other ways it's a lot younger."

I kissed his cheek. "Worried about our son, Dad?"

"Not worried. More like concerned. I don't want Taavi to make such an important life decision before he's ready."

"We're having Tia's parents over for dinner, not planning the wedding."

Noah folded the napkins in the shape of doves and placed a silver ring around each neck. "I'm guessing Tia's parents will grill us about the murders."

I nodded. "Tia mentioned their concern about her working in the sewing shop."

"I can't blame them for that. I'm still wondering if we should pull Taavi out of the fashion show."

"Taavi would consider that child abuse."

"Have you gotten any closer to figuring out the identity of the murderer?"

I glanced down at the now empty drawer of the hutch. "I've drawn a blank." After closing the drawer, I added, "But I did find out some new information." I giggled naughtily.

He held up a knife. "In the words of Martin, 'Gossip is like fertilizer. It should be spread all over as fast as possible, so stories can grow.'"

I chuckled. "Ulla Ultimate's personal assistant, Miles Jeffrey, is now in our show." I leaned against the hutch. "Our stage manager, Hoss Packer, saw Johnny Riley do something that Johnny didn't want him to see."

"What? Did Johnny accidentally cut off his arm with a sheering scissors?"

"Good one, but I have the feeling it was something else. I don't know what." *Perhaps commit the murders?*

Noah sighed. "Any news on Lila Hekekia?"

"Yes. She thinks Taavi's adorable and wants him to hurry and grow up so she can marry him."

"I take back what I said about Taavi and Tia not rushing into things."

I grinned. "Our son the little charmer overheard Lila on the phone to her producer."

"Her producer?"

I nodded. "Lila leads a secret life as Kona Lingus, the star of the porn movie *Cherry Seed*."

Noah nearly fell onto the window seat. "How did Taavi uncover *that*?"

"Taavi didn't know what he'd heard, but I put the celluloid pieces together."

Noah waved a fork in the air. "Given her career, and her willing affair with Tyler, she'll no doubt lose her sexual harassment case."

"Don't be so sure. Lila has the support of the God Loves Only the Rich Organization, the conservative press, and I assume every judge appointed by a Republican. She's not backing down unless she gets her own fashion show."

"Ulla Ultimate will never let that happen."

"To tipsy Tyler's chagrin." *Try saying that three times fast after going to the dentist.*

He rose and finished setting the table. "It appears that Ulla Ultimate and Tyler Greenway had a bumpy past."

"Their present isn't exactly a smooth ride either."

Noah and I headed to the kitchen where we prepared dinner: three bean minestrone, lobster ravioli, Caesar salad, roasted baby hens with fennel panzanella, and raspberry parfaits.

At six p.m. the doorbell rang (*to the tune of "Glitter and Be Gay"*). Taavi raced down the stairs faster than a conservative governor removing African Americans from the voter rolls. I opened the door feeling Noah's breath on my neck. "Welcome from all of us, Mr. and Mrs. Tedesco!"

Bill Tedesco, tall, thin, and bespectacled, offered a large hand. "Call me Bill."

"That's what *I* call him." Helen Tedesco burst out laughing and red ringlets danced around her full face. "Except if I've had a little too much to drink, and then I call him 'Bib.'" She giggled naughtily, and her chins giggled like gelatin during an earthquake.

"Hello, Helen." Noah shook her hand. "Call us Noah and Nicky."

Or Nicky and Noah.

"What a lovely home." Helen gave Noah the once-over. "And what a lovely man." She snickered wildly.

"Thank you." Noah smiled down at Tia. "And here's Tia, no doubt in need of some rest after doing so much sewing."

Tia, looking pretty in a cerise dress that complimented her long dark hair, greeted us. "Hi Mr. Abbondanza, Mr. Oliver. I'm not tired at all. I can't wait to see our fashions on the runway at the show."

Me too. If there are any models alive by then.

She mainlined it for Taavi. "Hi, Taavi."

He grinned at her as if they were the only two people in the room. "Hi, Tia."

Not texting or skyping, I wondered what they'd have to say to each other in person. My answer came soon enough.

"You look really cool, Tia."

"You look really cool too, Taavi."

"Thanks for helping me pick out the shirt, slacks, and blazer."

"They're really cool.

"Totally. Like your dress."

"Totally."

Clearly, they won't be collaborating on a novel to win a Pulitzer Prize.

Helen's rosy cheeks matched the rose pattern on her muumuu. "And don't you three boys look spiffy in your blazers."

Noah, Taavi, and I shared a smile.

Bill glanced down at his dark suit. "I came from work."

"Please come in." As we walked them down the hallway into our blue sitting room, I asked, "What do you do, Bill?"

"He puts up with me." Helen guffawed as she sat next to her husband on the powder blue sofa and took his hand. "I'm nuts about this guy. Or maybe I'm just nuts period." Hazel eyes bulged out of her head as she laughed uproariously.

It's going to be a long night.

Bill replied, "I'm chief financial officer at an investment firm."

Helen explained, "Remember when the Republicans deregulated all the finance laws and our tax dollars had to bail out the banks and moneylenders?"

Noah and I nodded.

"But the executives still got their big bonuses?" she added.

We nodded again.

"Bill was one of those guys."

"But after getting my bonus, I lost my job," he added.

I couldn't resist. "And here I thought show business was risky."

"But I got another position pretty quickly." He grinned. "At a higher salary."

Helen said, "And after the Democrats put back all the bank regulations, the Republicans did away with them again."

"Now I'm 'banking' on an even bigger bonus for this

government bailout," Bill said with a smile.

"I'll start saving up for it." I sat next to Noah on matching blue armchairs adjacent to the azure tiled fireplace.

Tia and Tava rested on the matching loveseat.

Helen blinked back tears. "How adult our kids look. In the fall, they'll be starting high school!"

"Very cool!" Taavi and Tia shared an anticipatory grin.

"I can't wait to star in the school plays," Taavi said.

Tia added, "I'll design the costumes!"

"Totally cool!" they said in unison.

I served iced tea with cinnamon and lemon while Noah offered everyone small plates, napkins, and forks for the appetizers on the coffee table: blue cheese and pear mini-tarts, mozzarella cheese with basil and balsamic vinegar, brie and crabmeat stuffed mushrooms, mascarpone cheese and spinach stuffed turkey meatballs, and artichoke hearts laced with goat cheese.

Helen cooed. "It all looks so wonderful. And it's all forbidden on my diet. I'm lactose intolerant."

Noah seemed upset. "We didn't know."

"No problem." Helen scooped a pill out of her purse and popped it into her mouth. "I just take one of these and I can eat anything and everything. And I usually do!" She giggled and helped herself to each appetizer.

Bill's brown hair fell over his brown eyes as he ate. "These are really good."

Helen groaned. "Bill can eat anything and not gain an ounce. I just glance at anything edible and I gain ten pounds." She chuckled. "So I do more than glance." Helen reached for another mushroom. "I just love a good mushroom head, don't you?"

"I sure do, Helen." I patted Noah's back. "And Noah loves a good mushroom head even more than me. Luckily I have one."

"You sure do!" Helen gobbled down another stuffed

mushroom.

Noah changed the subject. "Thank you all for coming."

"Our pleasure. We haven't seen you gentlemen since that *Nutcracker* dance show at the college." Bill pointed at Noah. "You were a terrific Cavalier."

"Thank you," Noah replied, always gracious.

Helen added, "And your white tights were to die for. I couldn't keep my eyes off them." She giggled again.

Noah blushed.

I jumped up and spun in the air. "I was the Mouse King."

Bill ate more of the appetizers. "I didn't recognize you."

I shrunk back into my seat. "I was wearing a mouse head."

"Good casting. Looking at the appetizers, it's clear you like cheese, Nicky!" Helen laughed so hard she choked up an artichoke heart. "And so do I!" She coughed up goat cheese. "Did I tell you I'm lactose intolerant?"

"Yes, you mentioned that," Noah replied.

Taavi rose and did a pirouette. "I played Fritz, the leading character."

A legend in his own mind.

As Taavi sat again, Tia said to her folks, "Taavi is a really talented singer, dancer, actor, and now model!"

"That's right!" Bill nodded in my direction. "We're looking forward to seeing your fashion show, Nicky."

"Need an extra model?" Helen laughed wildly.

Always courteous, Noah said, "We really appreciate all the fine work Tia has done in the sewing room."

"It's all she talks about," Helen said.

Noah replied, "I hear Tia gets her sewing skills from you, Helen."

Helen glanced at Tia's nearly empty appetizer plate. "Thankfully she doesn't get her appetite from me." She reached for another tart.

Bill's thin face saddened. "Now there's that murder

business. When Helen or I pick up Tia each night after rehearsal, there are always police officers and reporters swarming around the fashion building. To be honest, Nicky, we had considered not letting Tia go back there. But Tia promised us she'd be careful, and we know you guys are nearby."

I picked up my cue. "I'm working with the lead detective to catch the murderer."

Taavi cleared his throat. "I'm assisting with the investigation."

"As am I," Noah said.

"Me too!" Tia chimed as if Nancy Drew.

"Really?" Bill seemed worried.

I explained, "It takes a village (*of snoops*) to catch a murderer. You never know when someone might overhear something that cracks a case wide open. Just today, Taavi overheard a freshman fashion major say she is also—"

"Upset about not getting her own fashion show," Noah interjected.

Helen sighed. "Nicky and Noah, you are amazing!"

Finally interested in the conversation, I asked, "How so, Helen?"

"You are both so attractive and intelligent."

My future in-law!

Helen was on a roll (*no pun intended*). "And you act, direct, sing, dance, model, and even solve murder mysteries!"

Love her.

"You gay people are really something. No wonder you have special rights."

Cancel the wedding.

Noah shot me a silencing glance. "What special rights do you mean, Helen?"

She swallowed another mushroom. "You know, like how people can no longer say bad things on TV about gay people."

"I've heard some pretty bad things said about us on

conservative news and fundamentalist religious networks," Noah said.

Helen answered, "I meant how you can't fire gay people any longer."

I replied, "Actually, in half the states in the US, it's totally legal to fire someone, not hire somebody, or not rent an apartment to someone if they are gay, lesbian, or transgendered."

Her hazel eyes widened. "I didn't know that!"

My compassionate Noah gave her the benefit of the doubt. "Why should you? The media generally doesn't report things like that."

"Well they should!"

Noah explained, "Actually, Helen, in some red states it's legal for government-funded adoption agencies not to serve gay couples, due to the agencies' so-called religious beliefs."

Bill spoke up. "If somebody's religious beliefs preclude them from serving gay people, or any people, they should get the hell out the public service business. Go sell cakes or flowers at their church."

Helen laughed merrily. "*I* sell cakes at *our* church." She added quickly, "But I sold one to a nice gay man on Saturday." She exuded more pride than a Democrat at an equal rights march. "The man was African American too! He said he wanted to give his male partner a chocolate cream pie."

Noah buried his face in his napkin.

Bill slid to the edge of his seat. "This whole religious discrimination thing has gotten out of hand. People can practice their religion however they like, but they can't use their religion as an excuse not to serve someone in a hospital or restaurant."

"Tell that to the judges appointed by Republicans," I replied.

"I will." Bill was getting riled up. "And you people

should too. Why accept second-class status? If the African Americans did that, they'd still be sitting in the back of the bus, denied service at lunch counters, and using separate bathrooms, water fountains, and schools. *They* didn't take anyone's Bible-quoting religious bigotry, which resulted in the enactment of federal nondiscrimination laws based on race."

Always happy to flame the fans of drama, I said, "We've had a charge of religious discrimination in our own little fashion show."

"How so?" Bill seemed ready to call the ACLU.

"Lila Hekekia, the freshman fashion student who desires the spring spot for her own show, charged that Ulla Ultimate's show is discrimination against Lila's religious beliefs."

"How convenient for the student," Bill said with a grimace.

A wrinkle appeared between Helen's thinly tweezed eyebrows. "What in the show is against her religious beliefs?"

I smirked. "A black leather coat that Lila feels is too feminine for a man to wear." *Maybe she'll take it off in one of her porn movies.*

Bill pushed the large black glasses up his thin nose. "That's the problem with the world nowadays. Everyone thinks they can tell the other person what to do and not do." He waved a long finger at me. "Don't let this student get away with that religious discrimination flimflam, Nicky. These bullies win when people are complacent, don't vote, vote third party, or turn the other cheek. Your gay political groups are too weak. They accept defeat every time a Republican takes office. If the Republicans don't like you, stand up to them—in the ballot box, in their offices, and in front of their homes and businesses if necessary. Our tax dollars pay their salaries!"

And your bail-outs.

"They work for *us!*"

And the large corporations who bought them.

Bill seemed tenser than an altar boy summoned for private Communion with a priest. "I didn't rise to chief financial officer of my company, and the one before that, and the one before that, by sitting on my hands. I worked hard, squashed the competition, and fought like bloody hell to get ahead."

"I guess I've done the same thing." Helen giggled.

Noah asked, "Where do you work, Helen?"

She guffawed. "I don't have a job, except to take care of Bill and Tia."

I bit. "Then what did you mean about fighting to get ahead?"

"I fought for Bill!" She laughed wildly. "Bill and I met junior year of high school in biology class as lab partners. Our first assignment was to dissect a frog. My mother had taught me how to cook—including how to cut and clean a chicken. So, I assumed cutting a frog open would be a piece of cake. I also knew how to slice off a piece of cake." She giggled. "In any case, when I took the little knife on our lab table and split open the frog, Bill swayed back and forth like a politician in November."

"I think I was allergic to the formaldehyde," Bill interjected.

"I had learned to scrape out the organs of a chicken to make soup, so I did the same thing with the frog. As I dug in, Bill started to keel over. Gwendolyn Garrabaldi, a baton twirler, had her eye on Bill since seventh grade. She noticed Bill's decent and dove across the room to our table—her arms reaching out for Bill. Though I'd never played football, both of my brothers had, so I knew what to do. I tackled Gwendolyn to the floor, sprung to my feet, spread out my arms, and caught Bill just before he vomited—on my dress. He was so grateful, he asked me to the junior prom." She grinned. "They served frog soup, and Bill threw up on my gown. We've been inseparable ever since." She kissed Bill's cheek. "My frog prince and me."

Using his acting skills, Noah clasped his hands together. "What a beautiful story."

Bill rested his thin elbows on his narrow knees. "The point of Helen's story is that you can't sit idly by and watch other people take away what belongs to you." He waved his finger at Tia. "We've always taught Tia the ethic of hard work, sticking up for yourself, and claiming what's yours no matter who doesn't like it, and no matter what you have to do to hold onto it."

Since the conversation wasn't about Taavi, he squirmed in his chair. "Pop, can Tia and I go to my room and Skype with our friends?"

"All right. But be back down in half an hour for dinner."

Taavi and Tia flew up the flared oak staircase.

Helen smiled at us. "We're so lucky to have such wonderful children."

"On that we agree," Noah and I said in unison. *Aren't we adorable?*

The rest of the evening was pretty uneventful, except for when Helen laughed at my joke during dinner. Noah had to give her the Heimlich Maneuver, and a lobster ravioli flew out of her mouth like a cannon ball landing between two crystals in our dining room chandelier.

During dinner, I couldn't concentrate on the conversation as I pondered each fashion building murder, clue, and suspect.

After dinner, we wished the Tedescos goodnight—and then cleaned the chandelier. Noah and I tucked Taavi into bed, prying the cell phone from his hand. When my husband and I met in our skivvies at the center of our fourposter, he said, "Well, that was an adventure."

"Careful how you talk about our possible future in-laws." I wrapped my arms around the man of my dreams.

He rested his head against mine and I was happily lost in a strawberry patch. "Taavi's young. Tia may be the first of many."

"But I'll bet we won't forget her parents any time soon. They were real characters."

"They're probably saying the same thing about us."

"Good point."

Noah kissed my sideburn. "Do you think Manuello will let us rehearse in the fashion theatre tomorrow?"

I reached over to my night table and clutched at my phone. "I'd better make sure he's appeased the mayor and governor."

Moments later, Manuello's familiar growl filled my ear. I put him on speaker phone for Manuello stereo. He shouted, "I can't talk now, Nicky."

"Why? Is your wife on the extension? Relax, Manuello, she must have figured out our special relationship by now."

"Cut the comedy."

"*You're* the gay stand-up."

"We have another murder on our hands at the fashion building, and I'm knee deep in the coroner, police officers, forensics, and reporters."

"Without me!"

"Don't come here, Nicky."

"I will unless you promise we can rehearse in the fashion theatre tomorrow."

"You can rehearse tomorrow. I cleared it with the governor and the mayor. But you better solve this case soon!"

"How can I solve it if you won't tell me who was murdered?"

He sighed. "A fashion student. Lila Hekekia. An officer found her body behind a wide oak tree near the fashion building."

"What's the coroner's estimated time of death?"

"Three p.m."

Noah whispered to me, "That's shortly before Manuello finished his interviews in the fashion theatre lobby."

"Meaning someone involved in our show killed her," I replied.

Manuello said, "You got it, Mr. Director."

At the sight of Noah's pale face, I asked, "How was she killed?"

"A lighting instrument from your show struck her body in three places."

She had a killer body.

CHAPTER SIX

I woke groggily the next morning, yawning and rubbing my eyes.

Noah scooted over to me. "Poor Lila."

Wrapping my arms around my compassionate husband, I said, "You are a much better person than I." After placing my hands on his neck to bring Noah in for a good morning kiss, he cried out. "What's wrong?"

"It's sore there."

I felt Noah's neck and he flinched. Rising up on one elbow, I asked, "How long have your glands been swollen?"

"I didn't know they were."

Feeling his forehead, I said, "You aren't warm."

Noah pressed on his enlarged throat glands and winced. Then he checked under his armpits and at his groin. Terror filled his handsome face. "Nicky, they're all tender and swollen. Like my grandfather!"

I sat up. "Swollen glands can come from lots of things. Let's not panic." *I was panicking.* "But just to be on the safe side, I think you should call Dr. Jeff."

Noah had already reached for his phone on the night table and called Dr. Jeff. Thankfully there had been a cancellation, and Noah made an appointment.

While Noah was in the bathroom, I lay in bed with my laptop, searching anything I could find on swollen lymph nodes. The range of information was bountiful and vague.

Noah dressed quietly by the closet, deep in thought.

"It's probably nothing." I wasn't convincing either of us.

Finished dressing, Noah stood over my bed. "Let's not tell Taavi or anyone about this. No point worrying them."

I'm worried enough for everyone. I tried to sound calm. "Sure. If that's what you want."

He seemed more determined than I had ever seen him. "That's what I want." Noah headed for the door. "I'll make breakfast."

I scooted out of bed. "I can do it."

"I want to, Nicky."

Holding his hand, I said, "We'll get through this. We're Nicky and Noah."

He squeezed my hand and then left the room.

I thought about Noah as I showered, applied the anti-aging skin cream to my body, and dressed. When I got downstairs, I had a quiet breakfast (scrambled eggs with black truffles and pumpkin spice bread followed by vitamins with a cherry apricot smoothie chaser) in the nook, careful not to let Taavi notice my concern about Noah.

Then Noah sped us to the college, where we dropped off Taavi with Martin and Ruben in Martin's office. Next, Noah drove like a bat out of hell to Dr. Jeff's office.

After an exasperatingly long time in the waiting area, the nurse finally brought us into the examining room. She took Noah's temperature, weight, and blood pressure, and then sat at a side table to enter the results into the computer. Next, she handed Noah a robe, told us Dr. Jeff would be in shortly, and left the room. Noah took off his clothes and got into the robe with the tie at the back. Seated on the examining table, he held my hand as I sat on the chair next to him.

"Everything's going to be all right," I said, not totally believing it.

Noah squeezed my hand.

"It's probably something an antibiotic can knock out easily. And it was your grandfather who had lymphoma, not your father. Your dad's perfectly healthy and probably enjoying a cheese omelet right now while watching the movie *Mouse Hunt*." *Am I trying to convince myself or Noah?* "And even if you have lymphoma, which you don't, there are new methods of treatment now that weren't available during your grandfather's time. There's a much higher treatment success rate."

Dr. Jeff Solly finally entered, his shoulders stooped over in a three-piece gray suit. The tall, thin, bald, elderly man as usual had a compassionate look on his aging face.

Noah found his voice first. "Thank you for seeing me on such short notice, Dr. Jeff."

"It's always good to see you, young man." He stood next to the examining table. "I hear your lymph nodes have swelled up."

Noah nodded.

"How long has this been going on?"

I replied, "At least since early this morning."

"Are they tender to the touch?"

Noah nodded again.

Dr. Jeff asked, "Have you been lethargic lately? Sleeping more than usual?"

Noah shook his head.

"How's your appetite?"

"The same as before."

"Any change in bowel movements?" Dr. Jeff asked.

Again, Noah shook his head.

"Any disorientation? Night sweats?"

"The only symptom is the sore swollen lymph nodes." I blurted out. "Noah's grandfather died of lymphoma."

"Yes, I read that in the chart." He glanced at the computer screen in the room. "Your temperature, weight, and blood pressure are normal. So we can probably rule out bacterial infection. Sore, swollen lymph nodes can come from a long list of things. It means the lymph nodes are doing their job."

"Doing their job?" I asked.

Dr. Jeff nodded. "Filtering out something toxic in the body."

Like cancer.

"All right, young man. Let's have a look."

As Dr. Jeff examined Noah, I closed my eyes and offered a silent prayer. *God, Jesus, Holy Spirit, Buddha, Mohammed, Mother Earth, every god and goddess in the stratosphere, I need your help. You see, it took me quite a long time, but I finally found the man of my dreams, my perfect soulmate. I've never loved anyone like I love Noah. He's my husband and my life. We have a son together. I know a lot of people get sick, and their loved ones pray to you for help. And I haven't exactly been the kindest, worthiest, most noble person in the world. But Noah is. He's goodness, love, hope, and kindness all wrapped into one person. My person. My Noah. I'd say I don't want to live without him, but to tell you the truth — and I guess this is a good time to do that — I can't live without him. So please watch over us. Let this be easily treated. Don't let Noah be taken away from me. Please let him be well.*

Unable to stand it a moment longer, I asked, "What do you think it is, Dr. Jeff?"

He folded his long arms over his sunken chest. "Of course I'm concerned about the lymph nodes, given your family history. Since you both told me you are monogamous, after seven years together, I'm not worried about HIV. But we'll test for it just to be sure. The blood work will also check for a number of things."

"Such as?" Noah and I asked in unison.

Dr. Jeff patted our shoulders. "Let's not be concerned about that now. The nurse will take more blood than a vampire coming off a hunger strike." He smiled at Noah. "Since you have no other symptoms, put this out of your mind. Live your life as you did before. I'll phone you as soon as I know anything."

After Noah had dressed and given blood, I drove us back to campus. During the ride, we both agreed to forget about Noah's blood tests until we heard from Dr. Jeff with the results. *Easier said than done.*

We met up with Taavi, Tia, Martin, and Ruben in the rear of the fashion theatre house. With concern about Noah's health issue forefront in my mind, I welcomed the opportunity to leap back into director and detective modes. As an actor, Noah was capable of hiding his fear and acting (*pun intended*) as if nothing was wrong.

Tia, looking cute as a button (*literally*) in a button-down raspberry blouse and shirt, said, "Thank you for inviting us to dinner last night."

Always a gentleman, Noah said, "It was our pleasure."

She added, "My parents thought you were both really cool."

Noah smiled. "We thought they were pretty cool too."

As cool as hypothermia.

A solemn look overtook Noah's handsome face. "Taavi and Tia, there's been another murder. So I want the both of you to be very careful. Do you understand?"

Taavi and Tia nodded.

My best friend and department head looked as if he was about to burst out of his black leather skivvies. "I am absolutely beside myself about Lila Hekekia!"

I patted his small leather back. "Me too. I can't believe one of Manuello's stooges found her body instead of *me.*"

Martin slapped my shoulder. "That's not what I meant!"

"Of course it isn't." Always the font of decency, Noah said, "A young woman has been killed. We're all upset about it."

"That's not what I meant either!" Martin glared at me like an NRA member meeting a high school student at an anti-assault weapon rally. "You never gave me the dirt on her."

I covered Taavi's ears, and Noah covered Tia's. The two of them texted each other. I replied to Martin, "Lila Hekekia was also Kona Lingus, the star of the porn film *Cherry Seed*."

Martin was practically apoplectic. "How could you keep that juicy tidbit from me, Nicky!"

Ruben explained, "Martin didn't get his gossip fix of the day yet, so he's cranky."

"Well now you know about Lila." I tugged at my blazer. "But I can't figure out if that had anything to do with her murder."

"How was she killed?" Martin asked as if an afterthought.

I replied, "Manuello said she was hit with one of our stage lights."

Overhearing, Cory Ultimate joined our group. "So *that's* what happened to it. I'll have to replace the light before the tech rehearsal." He disappeared.

Noah threw up his hands. "Isn't anybody upset that a student was murdered?"

I pointed to Associate Professor of Fashion Tyler Greenway, sitting in the front row of the theatre with his head in his hands. "*He* seems to be suffering."

"I'm guessing he's suffering from a hangover, or a herpes outbreak," Martin said, clearly hoping for more gossip.

"Nicky, maybe you should see if he's all right." Martin nudged me forward.

I whispered to Noah, "Will you be all right?"

He nodded.

I made my way over to Tyler, his stocky build barely contained in an electric blue sweater and brown slacks. "My condolences about Lila."

Glancing up at me with sad eyes, Tyler said, "She was really talented. You should have seen her designs."

"I saw her designs—on you."

Tyler took a drink from his flask. "Lila was a student infatuated with her professor. I let my guard down one night. And the rest is sexual harassment case history."

"Which is now no more."

"I can't say I'm unhappy about that."

No surprise there. "Do you know about Lila's...other life?"

"The porn stuff?"

I nodded.

"She told me about it. I advised her to stop. She didn't listen to me."

Sitting next to him, I asked, "Do you think someone in the porn industry murdered her?"

"Why am I not surprised to hear that Lila Kekekia was a porn star?" Ulla Ultimate stood in the aisle next to us.

I glanced up. "I assume a great many things don't surprise you, Ulla."

"Including the demise of Lila's religious discrimination suit against your fashion show," Tyler added.

Ulla smiled victoriously. "Yes, the silver lining."

Tyler took a sip from his flask. "It's nice to see that some things don't change, Ulla."

"Such as?" She placed a hand on her hip.

"You're still the same cold, selfish bitch you were in college."

Ulla glared down at him. "Since both lawsuits are gone, why aren't *you*, Tyler?"

He stood and faced her. "After what you told me last night, I want to make sure *you* aren't suing me too."

"We both made our perspectives known on the subject. You're safe, Tyler." She glanced at the black leather watch on her thin wrist. "The liquor store in town is open by now. Why don't you go somewhere that interests you?"

Tyler wobbled away. As he brushed past Taavi, he said, "Don't ever get serious with a woman." Then he exited out the rear door with a slam.

"He's upset about Lila," I said.

"Is he?" Ulla faced me.

"Aren't you?"

"No." Glancing at the expression on my face, she added, "Did I shock you, Nicky? I've never seen the point in false sentiment. The girl got what was coming to her."

"Did *you* give it to her, Ulla?"

"Would I tell you if I had?" She adjusted her wig. "Are we ready for the tech rehearsal, Mr. Director?"

"I'll check with everyone backstage." After receiving a reassuring look from Noah, I mounted the steps and walked across the runway into the dressing room. Cory Ultimate was dressed in what appeared to be black leather straps draped around his body — barely covering the family jewels. Praying he wouldn't breathe and cause a costume malfunction, I asked him, "Ready to rehearse the kink section of the show?"

He nodded and thankfully nothing fell out of his outfit. "I replaced the light on stage, and the set looks good."

Miles Jeffrey came out of the bathroom in his black leather short shorts, chains, boots, and cap.

Ulla must give her assistant plenty of time off to work out in the gym. "Thank you for joining the show, Miles."

He smirked. "Ulla twisted my arm — literally."

Pointing to his bulging bicep, I replied, "And it looks none the worse for it. We'll start in five minutes." I left the room and then hovered in the hallway, peaking back inside.

Miles and Cory gazed at each other and then they burst out laughing.

"We're quite a pair," Miles said.

Cory grinned. "Actually, last night I had a dream about that."

"Being dressed in leather?"

Cory shook his head. "That we were a couple. Isn't that

a riot?"

Miles smiled. "Yeah."

"Of course, that could never happen. You think I'm a spoiled, arrogant child."

"And you think I'm a solemn, boring, prig."

Cory laughed. "The idea that you and I would be together is totally ridiculous, even in a dream."

"Agreed." Miles chortled.

Cory cleared his throat. "Have you found any more guys who don't want to date me?"

Miles rubbed his forehead. "You can relax. I think we've run out of prospects."

"What will my mother say?"

"She'll probably fire me."

Cory rested a hand on his shoulder. "That wasn't my intention."

"Wasn't it?"

"No. It isn't your fault I'm not loveable."

Miles sighed. "And it's not your fault I'm incompetent in my job."

"You're totally competent. Nobody could find a mate for me. I'm unmatchable."

Miles shrugged sadly. "Then I guess you'll be back to flirting with college guys, and I'll be getting my pink slip." He started walking away.

Cory blocked his path. "Wait. What if you and I went out on a date?"

"What would that prove?"

"That you can find me a conservative, stalwart date."

"Meaning *me*?"

Cory nodded. "I know it's a wild idea, but what other options do you have to keep your job and Mom off my back?"

Miles cocked his head. "You'd go out on a date with me?"

"Purely to save your job and my inheritance of course."

"Of course."

Cory looked at him sheepishly. "Could you stand going out with me?"

"I guess I don't have a choice." Miles thought about it. "All right, I'll pick you up at your dorm room at seven. Dinner and a movie."

Cory smiled. "It's a date."

I turned and headed toward the sewing room. Spotting Hoss Packer and Johnny Riley standing in a corner of the room, I watched from the doorway. Johnny, in a loose asparagus-colored turtleneck and gray slacks, looked like a child wearing his father's clothing.

Hoss leaned toward Johnny, and Hoss's pecs nearly burst out of his maize T-shirt. "Are all the alterations finished?"

Johnny nodded. "It's a good thing too." He held up ten bandaged fingers. "How's the show coming?"

"Fine. If I can get the sound and lighting cues right."

"You will."

You'd better!

Hoss smiled, revealing a row of straight white teeth. "This is nice."

"What?"

"Us...talking."

"I know. I can't believe it. I keep waiting for my dorm monitor to wake me up and tell me I overslept and missed my classes."

"This isn't a dream, Johnny." Hoss took his hand.

"Ow!"

"Sorry." Hoss gently kissed Johnny's hand.

"Why'd you do that?"

"Because I like you."

Johnny looked away. "You don't have to say that just to be nice."

"I'm not nice! I mean, I'm a nice guy, but I'm not being nice now."

"Yes, you are. As a matter of fact, I can't imagine you ever *not* being nice."

Hoss exhaled in frustration. "Johnny, I like you. A lot. And I'd like us to…see each other when the fashion show is over."

"I'm sure we'll run into one another on campus when school is back in session."

Wake up and smell the testosterone, Johnny!

Hoss placed a hand on Johnny's cheek. "Maybe this will explain what I'm trying to say." He planted a soft, sweet kiss on Johnny's lips.

Johnny gasped.

"Didn't I shave close enough?"

"You shaved fine."

"Then what is it?"

"I've never been kissed before. Except by my dog. And he did it to get a treat."

"Then let's try again." Hoss took Johnny in his strong arms and kissed him harder and deeper.

"I can't believe you did that!"

Hoss released him. "Too forward for you?"

Johnny shook his head back and forth like a windshield wiper on high speed. "No, I liked it. I *really* liked it. Almost as much as I liked the morphine they gave me in the hospital after I broke my collarbone when I accidentally ran my car off a cliff for the second time."

"Then what's the problem?"

"The problem was my broken collarbone. And my broken leg and shoulder from the first time I had accidentally driven my car off the cliff."

Hoss sighed. "I meant, what's the problem with me kissing you?"

"It's not a problem. At all! You're a terrific kisser. Much better than my dog."

"Then what's the issue?"

"The issue is…after what you saw me do, how can you

be interested in me?

"I've been interested in you for a long time, Johnny. And what I saw didn't change that one bit." Hoss giggled. "As a matter of fact, it made me want you even more."

A murder fixation?

Johnny lit up like fireworks watched by someone with a detached retina. "Do you really mean it?"

"I really mean it."

They shared a long, passionate kiss.

I went back into the house and took my front center seat. After I called out for everyone to take their places for the tech rehearsal, Hoss raced into the house and hurried into the lighting booth. We sat in darkness for ten minutes. Finally, the yellow then blue then eventually red lights came up on the stage. The models entered the runway in their kink outfits. Cory and Miles looked incredibly sexy — to each other. Noah's wardrobe was the most interesting: a takeoff on a black leather harness and sling. Always a trouper, he performed beautifully. Taavi looked quite comical in a black leather doggy outfit, which he milked to the bone (*pun intended*). Martin stole the show twerking in his black leather skivvies. When the set was over, the models disappeared backstage one at a time (*Taavi last of course*). The music changed to a country western tune. I yelled, "Hoss!" and the finale number finally blared through the theatre's speakers. One by one, the models entered the runway in black leather tuxedos as they sang and waltzed the finale number, "Fashion Ultimate Offers You a Big FU."

When the rehearsal was over, Ulla Ultimate leapt to her feet, happier than a Nazi when a Republican wins an election. "Bravo! Wonderful!"

I wrote more than a police officer writing traffic tickets on quota due date. Then after calling everyone into the house, I gave my directorial notes, followed by Noah giving his notes on acting and movement. Finally, I told the models to change clothes, go home, and get some rest.

Shortly afterward, Noah, Taavi, Martin, Ruben, and I sat on the tall leather chairs next to the cherry fireplace in Martin's theatre department head office. As usual Shayla sat at her desk in the outer office pretending to be working on her computer.

Martin straightened his mango-colored bowtie and sweater vest and then adjusted the mango monogrammed cloth napkin on his lap. "I was totally in my element on the runway."

"Yes you were."

Martin kissed his husband's cheek. "Thank you, Ruben."

"The 'element' of helium — that's why you were inflated." Ruben straightened the cuff of his mango leisure suit.

Shayla cackled from the outer office. "Good one, Ruben. I was thinking 'barium,' like the enema."

Martin seethed. "*You* are the element of arsenic, Ruben, toxic to my dreams."

I rested my china cup and saucer on the cherry end table. "All five models were terrific."

"Especially the youngest one," Taavi added, mid-text to Tia.

Noah sipped his hot cocoa. "And the technical blips will be fixed by show time."

"From your mouth to the tech gods' ears." I patted Noah's knee.

Shayla called out, "I thought Martin was God."

He hollered back, "I'm *your* god, Shayla, since I sign your paycheck today!"

"Love you, God Martin," Shayla replied.

Ruben nibbled on a finger sandwich. "Have you narrowed in on the killer yet, Nicky?"

"Are there any suspects still alive?" Shayla asked.

I rubbed my temples. "With Shane, Julio, and Cosmo

gone, Hoss Packer and Johnny Riley have gotten together. And it looks like Cory Ultimate and Miles Jeffrey may be headed in the same direction."

Noah added, "And with Lila out of the litigation picture, Ulla Ultimate and Tyler Greenway are lawsuit free."

"Not to mention happily free of each other," I added.

Taavi looked up from his phone. "Tia has been watching Tyler Greenway. She said he drinks and talks to himself a lot—about regretting something he did."

I nodded. "Your Nancy Drew may be on to something."

Noah slid to the edge of his chair. "Based on Tia's sleuthing, I'd like to do a role-play with Tyler."

I cocked my head. Noah's glance told me he needed to do it.

Martin rubbed his small hands together. "*I'd* like to have a crack at Hoss Packer."

No pun intended.

"Johnny Riley intrigues *me*," Ruben added.

I rested an arm around my comrades. "Let's put our heads together." (*It's not what you're thinking.*)

One hour later, having left Taavi with Martin and Ruben, I sat in a wooden booth at the Student Center building on campus. The two-story huge room was lined with more computer games than a department store in December. My non-alcoholic beer was as flat as the wooden table in front of me. A ping-pong table blocked me from the next table—unless I peeked over it.

A tall, thin, blonde woman with black eyes matching her black roots entered in a white pantsuit adorned with gold jewelry. *Noah?* After sitting at the booth next to mine, she, or rather Noah, glanced at the wooden clock on the wood paneled wall.

Associate Professor of Fashion Design Tyler Greenway appeared at the door and scanned the room. After taking a swig from his flask, he returned it to his inside jacket pocket. Then he staggered over to Noah's table. "Excuse me, are you Prima Dona Teller?"

"I am." He spoke in an accent somewhere between Italian and Mongolian.

"Professor Nicky Abbondanza phoned about our appointment. I'm Tyler Greenway."

Noah's deadpan expression didn't change. "Sit."

After Tyler was seated, he asked, "Would you like something to drink?"

Noah looked down his long nose at Tyler. "I never drink, eat, or sleep."

"What do you do?"

"I put all my energies into selling my clothes on cable television—next to a loud, overbearing, pushy salesperson who never stops talking." Noah's face was like granite. "But that's not why people buy my clothes."

"Why do they buy them?"

Noah's face was still immobile. "Because they look at me and they see my heart."

Tyler fidgeted in his chair. Given Tyler's bulk, Noah nearly toppled out of the booth. "I apologize, but I've never seen your clothing or your television show."

Again, Noah's face was like stone. "But when you look at me, you see my heart. Can you feel it?"

"Well, I—"

"Look at my face."

"I—"

"Feel my heart!" Noah didn't move a cell on his face. "Do you feel it?"

"All right! I feel it."

"Now you know me. But I don't know you. I don't see your heart."

Tyler ran a hand through his thick mane. "Why do you want to know me?"

"To sell your clothes."

It was Tyler's turn to nearly fall out of the booth. "*My clothes?*"

"My friend, Nicky Abbondanza, and his good-looking and talented husband, Noah Oliver, told me you designed the fashions for Ulla Ultimate. By the way, Nicky Abbondanza is a very funny man. Every time I think of him, I laugh—very hard." Noah's face was stationary.

Good one, Noah.

Tyler answered, "Back in college, Ulla looked at my sketches, and I believe she incorporated some of my ideas into her designs."

"How did she see your sketches?"

"We were dating back then."

Noah stared at him blankly. "That was a long time ago. Where are your *current* designs?"

Tyler shrugged. "I haven't been able to do any."

Noah rose.

"But my ideas are all in my head. I can put them down on paper for you."

Noah sat again. "All right, but first I need to see your heart."

"Excuse me?"

"For me to sell your clothes, I need to see and feel your heart." Noah's face was as immovable as a boulder. "Show me your heart, like I've shown you mine."

Tyler scratched at his sweater. "I don't know how."

"Do you love *me?*"

"I just met you."

"But you've looked into my heart. Do you love me?"

"You seem like a nice woman, a little stiff, but—"

"Our deal is off."

"All right." Tyler wiped the sweat from his brow. "I love you."

"I don't believe it."

Really, Noah?

Tyler placed a hand over his heart. "I love you!"

"Don't love me like your whore. Love me like your wife."

"I don't have a wife."

"Then love me like your sister."

"I don't have a sister either."

"How about a daughter?"

"No." Tyler grimaced.

"I don't trust anyone without a family."

Tyler sighed. "I found out yesterday I have a son."

Noah's right upper lip moved a fraction of an inch upward. "Who is your son?"

Tyler groaned. "I don't know why I'm tell you this."

"Because you love me. And you want me to sell your clothes to people with obsessive compulsive personalities and nothing else to do but watch television and max out their credit cards leading to bankruptcy. So talk."

"All right!" Tyler rubbed his forehead. "I don't know where to start."

"At the beginning. Before you loved me."

"When I was in college, I screwed around...a lot...with a lot of women. The last thing I ever thought about was having a family. I was totally wild."

"Me too. It was my passionate nature." Noah's face was stiffer than a porn star's erection after an injection.

"But I got a girl pregnant, and she didn't tell me."

"Why not?"

"She knew I didn't want a child. I had made that perfectly clear to her again and again." He hung his head. "She also knew I wasn't in love with her. I made that pretty clear too. Besides, I dumped her, like all the others, after graduation."

Noah said, "Your son must be a young adult by now."

"Yeah."

"Have you met him?"

Tyler nodded.

"Do you love him more than you love me?"

Tyler shouted, "I don't love him at all. I think he's a spoiled, selfish brat who is as arrogant as his mother."

"Who is his mother?"

"Ulla Ultimate."

Cory Ultimate is Tyler Greenway's son!

"Have you told anyone else about this?"

"Yeah. A young woman I was involved with. I'm ashamed to admit, she was my student."

Lila Hekekia.

"Did you love this young woman more than you love me?"

"No, I didn't love Lila."

"What did Lila say about you having a son?"

"She mocked me, threatening to use my son in her sexual harassment suit against me. She said Cory is as much of a mess-up as his father, and she thought Ulla made the right decision not to tell me about him for all these years."

"That must have made you not love her."

"You're right. It made me hate her."

"So you killed her?"

"No!"

"You must tell me the truth if you want me to sell your clothes in tackily decorated TV studios."

"I'm telling you truth. I didn't kill Lila, or anyone." He clenched his fists. "Though I certainly thought about it."

Noah finished the meeting with false promises of selling Tyler's clothes—if Tyler ever designed them. After Tyler wobbled out, Noah and I headed over to the theatre building, where Noah changed his clothes, and I filled in a salivating Martin about Cory's paternity. Then Noah drove Taavi home, no doubt faster than a liberal signing a petition against animal abuse.

Still worried about him, I was proud of Noah for doing his role-play under challenging circumstances. As I walked across the campus replaying in my head what Tyler had said, the sun was low in the sky, its warm rays turning the white stone to glowing amber. I eventually found myself at the fashion building. After entering through the back door, I checked in with Hoss Packer, who was working in the lighting booth. I heard voices coming from backstage. So I headed up and across the runway to backstage, where I glanced into the sewing room. Johnny Riley and Tia were working on their sewing machines. I said, "Tia, I thought you had gone home?"

"Taavi's dog collar ripped." She held it up. "How does it look now?"

"Fetching (*pun intended*). When are your parents picking you up?"

She glanced down at her phone. "Now!"

"Good. You shouldn't be alone in here."

Johnny repaired a vest. "I've been watching over her. Owww!"

"Better bandage your nose, Johnny."

"Will do, Professor."

Tia texted Taavi, and then she left through the sewing room door.

I stood at the doorway, waved to Tia's mom, and then watched until the car drove off. Moving back to the hallway, I spotted Ulla and Cory in the dressing room. So I hung back and observed.

Cory's face was as red as the tank top barely containing his muscles. "I went for a drink in the Student Center. I overheard Professor Greenway in a nearby booth — talking to some blonde woman."

"That sounds like Tyler." Ulla sneered.

"Greenway told her something incredible."

"That I stole his designs in college?"

"That and how he impregnated you in college!"

Ulla rested her head in her hands. "I was afraid this would happen."

"Obviously not afraid enough to tell me about it!"

She sighed. "Why couldn't you have left this alone?"

"Because Tyler Greenway is obviously my father! A father who called me 'a spoiled, selfish brat who is as arrogant as his mother.' Can't say I disagree with him there." He turned on Ulla. "All the times I asked you! When I was a scout. Parents' Day at school. In bed crying myself to sleep at night. You never said a word. Were you ever planning to tell me this little tidbit about my life? How about if I needed an organ or bone marrow transplant? Would you have told me then?"

"Stop acting like a child."

Cory gasped. "'Stop acting like a child?' Is that all you have to say to me after keeping the identity of my father a secret from me for nineteen years!"

She rubbed her eyes. "Did you speak to Tyler about this?"

He nodded. "I confronted him outside the Student Center. I told him I knew the truth, and I asked if we could get to know each other." Cory held back tears. "Greenway said, 'In the animal kingdom, males may never know their offspring. Not altogether a bad idea.'"

What a snake — literally.

"What happened next?"

"I told Greenway he'd never be a father to me. He said that suits him just fine, since I'm such a 'bastard.'" Cory blinked back tears. "Mom, why didn't you tell me?"

"Isn't it obvious?"

"Not to me!"

Ulla sat at a makeup table. "I was trying to protect you."

"From what?"

"You wanted so much to speak with your father. As the old expression goes, 'Careful what you wish for.'" Rising, she took his hand. "Cory, Tyler was a selfish, conceited, manipulative, lying, womanizer in college. I can't explain why I fell in love with him, or why I still think about him."

"Is that why you read your old diary at night?"

She nodded sadly.

"Why didn't you tell Tyler you were pregnant back then?"

"Because he made it crystal clear that he wanted nothing to do with having a family. When I finally told him about you, I realized he hadn't changed on that score. I wanted to spare you the demoralizing hurt I felt after speaking with him."

"I'm accustomed to it, Mother. I've been rejected by you for my entire life."

She placed a hand on his cheek. "I know I haven't been the best mother. I worked too hard, and I expected you to grow up too fast. When you failed to reach my unreasonable expectations, I was critical and domineering. But I never for one moment regretted having you. And regardless of what I say or do, I love you so much, and I'm incredibly proud of you. Please don't let Tyler Greenway upset you or come between us. He never wanted a wife or child, and I truly believe you and I benefited from that decision. I didn't want to lie to you about your father. So I said I nothing. I realize now that was a huge mistake. But we can't go back in time. We can only move forward. And we're both better off without Tyler Greenway in our lives." Ulla raised her arms toward her son.

He ran out of the dressing room.

I made my way back into the theatre. Hoss had left (*hopefully having solved all the lighting and sound problems*). I sat and enjoyed the dark stillness of my favorite place. Eventually, I continued out the back door. At twilight, the campus was deserted, the buildings looking like cobalt cut-outs. I walked along the cobblestone path fenced in by the low now gray stone wall. Then I tripped over a flask. Picking it up, I removed the top and noticed a white stain that smelled like bleach. In my peripheral vision, I spotted what looked like a hand reaching out from under a bench. Bending down, I realized it was Tyler Greenway. *Drunk?* I reached for his arm and didn't find a pulse. Upon further examination, I found the same white stain on his lips. *He's dyed!*

When I placed my finger under his nose and didn't feel a breath, I reached for my cell phone to call Manuello. It was dead. So I ran back to the fashion theatre and entered through the back door. The theatre was still completely dark—except for the beautiful blonde woman in white floating on the stage. As I raced toward her, I banged into the back of a chair and toppled over it. *Black out.*

CHAPTER SEVEN

In our T-shirts and boxers, Noah and I rested in our fourposter.

I'm not sure who had found me unconscious in the fashion theatre earlier, but somebody had evidently phoned the EMTs who had raced me to the emergency room. There I had been pronounced loopy for running around a dark theatre, but physically fine. So Noah, with Taavi riding shotgun, had sped me home from the hospital quicker than the NRA buying a conservative politician. The moment we had arrived, Taavi had headed for his room to text Tia. *No sympathy for the injured!* Noah had insisted I go right to bed—with him. After my loving husband had brought me a snack in bed which I had devoured, he had placed the tray on his night table and then climbed in next to me.

I rested my back against the pillows. "We're quite a pair."

He kissed my cheek. "The best pair."

My cell phone rang. I reached for it on top of my night table. "Nicky Abbondanza, cozy mystery solver."

"Are you delirious? What's that about a 'cozy mystery'?"

"Hello, Manuello." Noah motioned to me and I put Manuello on speaker phone. "Don't get any ideas, Manuello. I certainly won't get cozy with *you*, no matter how many times you ask me."

Manuello sighed. "I heard you took a fall."

"Worried about me?"

"Disappointed you're conscious."

I giggled. "I see through your brash, obnoxious, callous, incompetent, and dim-witted demeanor, Manuello. Deep down in your enlarged heart, I know you adore me."

He groaned. "My officers found the body outside the fashion theatre. Unfortunately, it wasn't yours."

"What did forensics give as the approximate time of death?"

"About eight p.m."

"That's shortly before I found the body."

"So that's why your prints were on Tyler Greenway's flask."

"Any other prints sharing it with mine?"

"No. Not even fingerprints want to be near you, Nicky."

"Is that another joke for your act?"

He exhaled loudly into the phone and my sideburn nearly bristled. "Will you stop talking about my comedy act!"

"Well somebody has to. Here you are ready to premiere as a gay comic and what I've heard so far hasn't been very promising. Unless you're a female music icon, sassy drag queen, a Democratic vice president, or a straight actor playing a gay role on TV, a gay audience can be really tough."

"Nicky, let me say this one last time. I'm no comedian."

"I know that! Why do you think I'm so concerned about your plans to tour the country telling lame gay jokes?"

"You're exasperating, you know that?"

"Yet you can't seem to get enough of me."

"I've had enough of you."

"So you phone me at night while I lay next to my husband in bed."

Manuello gasped. "Were you and Noah…?

I moaned. "Noah, don't stop. Please don't stop!"

Noah slapped my shoulder.

Manuello cleared his throat. "I know what you're doing, Nicky."

"I'm proud of you, Manuello. Especially since I can't imagine your wife has ever said that to you in bed."

"Which? 'Don't stop,' or 'I know what you're doing'?"

"Both I imagine."

"You and Noah aren't really having sex."

"Did you plant a camera in our bedroom? I know you fantasize about me in bed, Manuello, but this time you've gone too far."

He groaned. "I get it. You're pretending to have sex with Noah, so I'll be embarrassed."

"You're right there, Manuello. Since you caught me, now we'll do it for real." I cried out, "Noah, stop! Not while I'm on the phone."

Manuello sighed. "I know you're faking it, Nicky."

Noah shook his head at me.

Undeterred, I bellowed, "Noah! How did you fit it all in! Noah, that feels so good. I...I'm going to..."

"Okay! I believe you and Noah are having sex!"

"Well of all the homophobic insults! Just because we are gay, you think we do nothing but have sex! I'm offended, Manuello. Your new gay boss will be too when I tell him."

"Nicky, you better tell me how you found the body, or I'll haul you off to jail."

"Where you will no doubt force me to take a shower with you and drop the soap."

"Nicky!"

Noah motioned for me to tell Manuello.

"All right. I'll take pity on you, Manuello, and, as usual, do your job for you."

"Talk, Nicky."

I said into the phone, "After finding out that Cory

Ultimate is Tyler Greenway's son—"

"How did you find that out? Never mind. I don't want to hear tales of your freaky dress up interviews. Go on."

"I walked across the campus and found Tyler Greenway laying under a bench with bleach in his flask—and over his lips."

"How did you know it was bleach?"

"Bleach has a distinct smell. They really should teach you these things in detective school, Manuello."

"Keep going."

"Since my cell phone was dead, I ran back to the fashion theatre. That's where I saw the ghost again."

"The ghost?"

"A beautiful blonde woman in a white gown."

"*You* had visions of a beautiful woman?"

"I can appreciate a beautiful woman in the same way you appreciate me, Manuello."

"Who's the woman in white?"

"You got me. Well, not literally. So don't get any ideas."

"Is that it, Nicky?"

"Just that, since I'm wounded in action saving your job by doing my own investigation, you can send me flowers and candy."

"You can kiss my ass."

"Another sexual fantasy about me! What's next? Are you going to ask what I'm wearing? A T-shirt and boxers, if you must know."

"How about if I box *you*?"

"Manuello, I certainly hope you won't be putting that sour joke in your act."

"How about if I put my fist up your—?"

"Yet another sexual fantasy about me! Manuello, you have a wilder imagination than a conservative news anchor."

"You want reality, Nicky? How's this? Your fashion

show isn't opening in two nights."

"Then when is it opening?"

"It isn't."

Noah shared my worried glance.

"Manuello, if we can't open, I won't be able to deliver the killer to you."

"Why is that always the case?"

"Because I need to watch all the suspects under the illuminating lights of my show. Let us open as planned, and I'll snag the culprit."

"I'll need to beg and plead to the mayor and governor again. And if they say yes, you better not disappoint me."

"Have I ever?"

"I refuse to answer that."

"Why?"

"Because whatever I say, you're going to put some gay spin on it."

"Gay spin? Do you mean like a gay ice skater?"

"You know what I mean."

"Yes, Manuello, we've come so far in our intimate relationship that, like other couples, we know what the other is thinking before he even voices it."

"What am I thinking, Nicky?"

"That you love me. And you want to tell me what happened when you interviewed the suspects."

I heard papers shuffling.

"Sometime before the murder, Cory Ultimate, Ulla Ultimate, and Miles Jeffrey each individually argued with the victim about Cory's paternity, while Johnny Riley and Hoss Packer each went for a walk on campus—alone."

"And all five of them told you they know nothing about Tyler Greenway's murder."

"Exactly."

"See, we think alike."

"Get some rest, Nicky. The next two days are hopefully going to be eventful."

"Pleasant dreams, Manuello. But not about me!" I placed the phone back on the night table.

Noah wrapped his arms around me. "How's your head?"

"They're both feeling a bit sluggish." I kissed his neck and he flinched. "Throat glands still sore?"

He nodded.

"How about the others?"

"No change."

I pulled him in closer. "Tomorrow we'll hear from Dr. Jeff and everything will be all right. You'll see."

Noah nodded, blinking back tears.

As I hugged him tightly, I silently reminded the gods how much I needed their help.

My headache was gone the next morning, but a purple bruise continued to grace my forehead. After I showered and applied my anti-aging cream, I combed my hair over the bruise. Then I dressed and headed downstairs to the breakfast nook, where Noah served sweet potato waffles with asparagus quiche and a banana papaya smoothie, and a hoard of vitamins—for both of us. I asked him, "Any word from Dr. Jeff?"

He sighed. "I phoned, and the nurse said the results aren't all back yet."

"Do you mind if I go to the gym?"

"Are you feeling okay?"

I nodded, making sure my hair covered the bruise.

"Then please, go. There's no reason for you to be a prisoner here."

Taavi came downstairs and joined us for breakfast. Tia (via Skype) offered me her well wishes. After thanking her, via Taavi, I whispered in Noah's ear, "Call me the second you hear anything."

He whispered back, "Of course."

I kissed my two men goodbye, and then I drove to the gym on campus. Generally, a work-out exhausts my body but stimulates my "little gray cells." However, my little gray cells seemed just as pooped as my body after I finished a session on the elliptical machine followed by working out my pecs, biceps, and triceps with hand weights. By the time I finished crunches for my abs, I was crunched out.

I made my way over to the fashion theatre. It was a beautiful spring day, but with Noah's condition on my mind, I hardly noticed. I passed Manuello's officers and then opened the rear door of the fashion theatre. Noticing Johnny Riley sitting in the lighting booth with Hoss Packer, I moseyed over and stood at the open doorway. Johnny's thin body was encased by Hoss's powerful bulk as they shared a long, passionate kiss. When I cleared my throat, they separated like a politician and their campaign promises in December. I asked, "Are you guys ready for the tech run?"

Hoss straightened his jonquil T-shirt. "The lighting and sound cues are all entered into the computer, Professor."

Hopefully in the right order.

Johnny scratched at his moss flannel shirt. "The wardrobe is all hung up in the dressing room, Professor."

Hopefully the models aren't hung as well. You know what I mean. I leaned on the door. "By the way, did either of you see Professor Greenway at any time last night?"

Johnny shook his head, and auburn hair filled the lighting booth.

"I didn't see him either," Hoss said.

"But we heard about what happened to him." Johnny's teeth chattered. "Is it safe being in this theatre? I'm beginning to fear for all of our lives."

Hoss wrapped his muscular arm around him. "Don't

worry. I'll protect you."

Johnny released into Hoss and they kissed again.

Is this a theatre or a motel? I continued up the runway to the backstage area. Peeking into the dressing room, I found Cory and Miles in their opening activewear outfits.

Miles asked him, "Are you all right?"

Cory sighed. "I was up most of the night…thinking."

"What did you think?"

"About Tyler Greenway. Even though he dumped on me, I'm sorry about what happened to him."

Miles nodded. "I'm sure what he said hurt you, but you've lived nineteen years without a father, and you survived. So, what have you really lost?"

"Good point, Miles." Cory smiled. "I like this."

"What?"

"Us not arguing."

"Me too." Miles returned the smile.

"I know the only reason we went out was to save your job, but I have a confession to make: I had a good time."

Miles scratched his head. "So did I."

Cory grimaced. "You don't need to sound so surprised."

"I'm not. It was nice."

Cory did a doubletake. "You really enjoyed being with me?"

"Yes."

"You're just being polite."

"Actually, I'm not." Miles cleared his throat. "I have a confession to make too. I didn't realize it at the time, but while I was interviewing all those guys, I was subconsciously hoping they wouldn't want you."

"How come?"

"Because I found someone, to his surprise, who is *very* interested in you."

Cory sniggered. "I pity the poor guy. He must be a real loser. Who is he?"

"Meet the real loser."

"You?"

Miles nodded. Then he leaned in and planted a soft, sweet kiss on Cory's lips.

Cory gazed into his eyes. "Miles?"

"Yes?"

"Do me a favor?"

"What?"

"Don't look for any more guys for me."

"Okay."

They shared another kiss, deeper, longer, and more intense than the first.

Awwwww.

"Wow." Cory caught his breath. "Where do we go from here?"

"Hopefully out to dinner again tonight?"

"Sure." Then Cory cringed. "Miles, I just thought of something. What if my mother doesn't approve of you?"

"She hired me."

"I mean, approve of you for *me*?"

"She'll probably fire me."

"Are you willing to risk your job over me?"

"Depends how dinner goes tonight."

They shared a chuckle.

Miles wrapped his arms around Cory's broad back, and Cory placed his hands on Miles' wide pecs. Cory said, "I'm glad you're in the show. Thank you for trying something new."

"Thank you for trying something new last night: a date that ended simply with a goodnight kiss at your door."

"The kiss was worth the wait. But we didn't get it totally right. So we need to try again."

They kissed. And they kissed again. And again.

Cory said, "Fair play. You planned our first date, so I get to decide what we do on our second date."

"And what's that going to be?"

"Let's just say, we won't be leaving my dorm room." Cory ran his hands down Miles' broad back to his bubble butt and squeezed.

They shared a longer kiss.

When they finally came up for air, I entered the dressing room. "Ready for our final tech run?"

Miles shrugged. "As ready as I'll ever be."

Cory placed an arm around his waist. "This guy will be terrific in the show."

"I never thought I'd be a model, or Cory's bodyguard." Miles shuddered. "This place has become a war zone."

I seized the opportunity. "Were you Cory's bodyguard last night?"

Miles cocked his head. "What do you mean?"

"When you spoke with Tyler Greenway."

Cory did a doubletake. "You talked to that creep?"

So much for not speaking ill of the dead.

Miles answered Cory. "After we ran into each other outside, and you told me about what Tyler had said to you, I confronted Tyler myself."

"What did he say?" Cory asked.

"The same crap he had told you." Miles grimaced. "Some people shouldn't be allowed to breed."

I asked, "What happened next?"

"Tyler took a swig from his flask and slithered away."

Cory clenched his fists. "If I ever have a kid, I'll love them no matter what the circumstances."

"And I'll make sure you do."

Cory and Miles shared a smile.

"Am I going to be a grandmother?" Ulla Ultimate strutted into the room wearing a black leather pantsuit. She asked Miles, "Have you found my son a potential husband? Remember, I must approve of your choice."

Cory and Miles stared at each other. After shuffling from black leather shoe to shoe, Miles finally mumbled, "I think I found someone right for Cory."

She grinned. "Speak up, Miles. Who's the lucky young man?"

Miles averted her glance. "I am."

"Excuse me?"

Cory's voice broke. "Mom, Miles and I are...sort of dating."

Ugh-oh.

She homed in on Miles. "*You're* dating my son?"

Miles nodded meekly.

"I hired you as my personal assistant to find my son a good match, and you are dating him yourself? That's like a butcher eating his own meat."

No pun intended.

"I can explain." Miles pulled back his shoulders. "When I was interviewing the various candidates, deep down I seemed to be happy when they weren't interested in Cory."

"Because your hidden plan was to nab my son — and his eventual inheritance — for yourself?"

"No." He gazed at Cory and smiled. "I think subconsciously I fell in love with Cory the moment I met him."

"And I fell in love with Miles."

Awwww.

Cory took his mother's hand. "Maybe that's one of the reasons I flirted with the other guys: I didn't want to face my true feelings for Miles."

Ulla was taken aback. "I thought you acted out to get back at me for working so much."

"That too." Cory took her hand. "And I'm sorry, Mother."

Miles confronted his boss. "If you're going to be angry with anyone, Ulla, be angry with me. I started things with Cory."

Cory added quickly, "And I was happy he did."

Ulla eyed the two young men up and down.

Miles asked, "Well, am I fired?"

"No." She smirked. "At least not yet."

"What do you mean?"

"Let's see how you treat my son. Then I'll decide if you still work for me." Ulla turned to me. "Nicky, do you want something?"

I remembered my investigation. "Ulla, did you speak with Tyler last night?"

"Yes. Cory had told me something that disturbed me."

"About his parentage," I replied.

She was clearly surprised. "You know about that?"

Cory smirked. "Good news travels fast."

I explained, "Like Cory, I overheard Tyler talking in the Student Center."

She folded her arms over her chest. "I confronted Tyler outside the theatre. As usual, he dismissed me. So, I went back to my hotel suite."

I said to Ulla and Cory, "I found Tyler's body. I'm sorry for your loss."

"The memory of Tyler has kept me captive far too long." Ulla took Cory's hand. "My son and I lost many good things over the years. I realize now Tyler Greenway wasn't one of them. I hope Tyler rests in peace, and he lets us do the same. I bear the blame for my son's problems, and I hope I can make that up to him after the show."

Cory asked, "What happens after the show?"

She held her head high. "I've decided to take a break from Ultimate Fashion, and finally connect with the only person I love—my son. I think it's about time. Don't you?"

Cory's eyes filled with tears. "Do you really mean that?"

"I've never been more certain of anything in my life." Ulla opened her arms to him, and Cory rested his head on her black leathered shoulder. After patting his back, she wiped his eyes with her black leather handkerchief, and kissed his cheek. "I'm so sorry, Cory."

"I'm sorry too, Mom."

They embraced again.

Noah, Martin, and Taavi entered the dressing room, quickly changing into their opening outfits. Taavi said, "Tia's finished with all her sewing. Can she watch the tech run in the house, Pop?" He winked at me. "There's one model she's especially interested in checking out."

"Ruben is in the house as well." Martin sighed. "But the only thing he'll be checking is his pulse."

I mussed Taavi's hair. "Sure, Tia can watch the run." I whispered to Martin, "And I hear Ruben's pulse, and something else, rises every time you walk onto the runway."

Martin giggled. "The old fool has always been mad about me."

Or at least mad. I squeezed Noah's hand, wished everyone a good rehearsal, and then left to take my front center seat in the house. With my pad and pen in hand, and an offering to the runway gods, I called out for the tech run-through to begin.

After Ulla and Tia took their seats in the house, Hoss hit the first sound and light cues. The opening number began. I held my breath as the five models strutted their stuff in activewear. The combination of Martin's boundless energy and arthritic knees caused him to look like a marionette operated by a puppeteer on magic mushrooms. Taavi used the cute kid factor to the fullest. Despite Noah's concern about his test results, he was the epitome of masculine beauty and grace. Cory was a hot, hunky, hellion. *Try saying that three times fast without blowing out a candle.* Surprisingly, Miles was charismatic, sexy, and seemed quite at home on the runway. The clubwear, nightwear, casualwear, bathing suits, kink, and tuxedo sections went equally well, as did the intermission and finale numbers. A few lighting and sound cues faltered — including when we sat in the dark longer than the northeast blackout of 2003. Some choreography looked more like a telethon than a dance. We also experienced a costume malfunction when Miles' stick slipped out of his chap. However, all of the errors were fixable—after a long notes session with the models in the front of the house.

When we were through, Ulla stood in the aisle. "The show is wonderful, everyone. And it's even more wonderful to have my son here with me."

Cory blew her a kiss.

Tia raced over to Taavi. "You were totally cool!"

Taavi basked in her adoration. "It's so cool that you liked it!"

"Did you get my texts?"

He nodded happily. "During each costume change."

Martin sauntered over to Ruben in the second row. "Wasn't I astounding?"

"I was definitely astounded, Martin."

Martin kissed his husband.

After Johnny repaired Miles' chaps in the sewing room, we all ate a late lunch in the college cafeteria. Then Cory took Ulla back to his dorm room. Miles headed to the fashion theatre to rehearse his choreography. Tia's mother picked her up.

Noah ushered Martin and Ruben to the Theatre Department building's costume and makeup lofts to prepare our best friends for their upcoming role-play performances. I remained in the cafeteria with Taavi and spoke to Hoss Packer and Johnny Riley—laying the groundwork for our last two role-plays.

Once Noah drove Taavi home, I hightailed it over to a sitting room in the college dormitory. Unlike the beaten-up recreation and media rooms for the students, the reception space for visitors was painted pristine white with a marble ivory fireplace mantel as the centerpiece. Floor-to-ceiling windows welcomed the sun and passersby. I hid behind a white oak bookcase just as Hoss Packer walked in and sat on a vanilla overstuffed armchair.

A few moments later, a small, thin, ancient woman entered, wearing a mauve designer suit, a short dark wig, and large round glasses. There was so much gold jewelry around her neck, I couldn't fathom how she stood stationary. *Try saying that three times fast while eating peanut butter.* Except, it wasn't a she. It was my best friend and department head, Martin Anderson.

Hoss leapt to his feet. "Ms. Channel?"

"Call me, Cuckoo. Everyone does." Martin was going for French, but his accent sounded like a Swede speaking under a tsunami. "Come sit in Cuckoo's nest." He rested on an eggshell sofa. "You must be Horse Package."

He sat again on the armchair opposite. "It's Hoss Packer."

"Ah, I thought it was 'horse,' as in, 'He's hung like a racehorse owned by a gay royal,' and 'package' as in, 'His full package slid into the hole.'"

"It's Hoss Packer." His muscles rippled under the T-shirt.

Martin grinned. "Well, Hoss, you look more fertile than a teen in an abstinence-only program."

"I work out at the campus gym."

"Working out is wonderful. I sit on the stationery bicycle for spinning. Nobody can spin a tail…or tale like me." Martin gagged with laughter.

The theatre student scratched at the tight black hair on his head. "Professor Abbondanza set up this appointment."

"Yes, Nicky and I go way back—to when we danced in the chorus together on Broadway."

The chorus?

Hoss did a doubletake. "I didn't know Professor Abbondanza sang and danced in the chorus."

"My, yes. Nicky took his place in the line of chorus boys and bent over, lifted his legs over his head, and shook his bootie big time!" Martin unleashed a laugh that sounded like a fox trying to impregnate a woodpecker.

"When we did *The King and I*, Nicky forgot to wear a dance belt under his tights. The Siamese children really meant it when they sang, "Getting to Know You." During the run of *Singin' in the Rain*, Nicky had a bit too much to drink before one performance, and the rain dance became a golden shower."

Martin!

He was on a roll. "Nicky was so nelly in 'Sit Down You're Rockin' the Boat,' the critics nicknamed the show *Gays and Dolls*."

So help me!

"Nicky spun the leading lady too hard, and the show became *Goodbye, Dolly*. He lifted a female dancer too high and *Kinky Boots* became *Kinky Boobs*."

Get to the questions, Martin!

Hoss cleared his throat. "Professor Abbondanza said you're looking for a new floor manager."

"Yes!" Martin pushed the humungous eyeglasses up the tiny bridge of his narrow nose. "My hardwood floors at home are in terrible need of a good waxing. You see my husband is quite elderly, and he doesn't move very well. When I push him across the floor, he skids like a pebble skimming a lake overgrown with algae." He smiled nostalgically. "In the old days, I'd give Herman a good whack and he'd slide across the floor like a sleigh on thin ice. To the dining room, bedroom, bathroom, wherever I shoved him."

Not floor waxer, Martin, floor manager!

Hoss cocked his head. "Ms. Channel—"

Martin wagged a wrinkled, brown-spotted finger at him. "Please, I'm Cuckoo!"

No argument here.

"Cuckoo, I'm currently the stage manager for Ulla Ultimate's fashion show that Professor Abbondanza is directing at the college."

"Ulla's a horrible designer! All that black leather makes me think of dungeons, masters, slaves." He grinned.

"Not altogether a bad thing now that I think about it."

Hoss leaned forward, and his pecs nearly exploded out of his T-shirt. "I understood from Professor Abbondanza that you were seeking a floor manager for your upcoming television show."

"Of course! My upcoming fashion show on the Cuckoo Channel. I'll be showing clips of how other designers are dressing celebrities." Martin displayed yellow molars. "Then I'll rip them to shreds!"

Hoss asked, "The designers, the celebrities, or the clothing?"

"Yes." Martin pointed at Hoss and his jewelry jangled, sounding like a reindeer during an avalanche. "So I need a good floor manager to sweep up the debris. After all, I'm a sterile Cuckoo."

Hoss scratched his chin. "I thought a television floor manager gives information from the director in the control room to the crew on the studio floor and back again."

"That too. And my director likes lots of gossip." Martin pursed his chapped lips. "Are you up for that?"

Hoss smiled at the possibility. "I'd love to get into television. And I'm certainly not a fan of A-list people in the fashion industry."

"How fitting. Get it?" Martin laughed wildly.

Get to the investigation!

"Hoss, this may be your only shot at a career in television. Care to aim the gun?"

"Are you offering me the job?"

"Not so fast." Martin took a compact from his purse and applied white powder to his pale face. "I need some proof."

"Proof?"

"That you despise the fashion industry — except for *my* clothes of course."

"I do."

"Do tell."

Hoss's cheeks turned pink. "I don't talk to many people about that."

"Good, because 'many people' aren't Cuckoo Channel, handing you a job in television."

"My story is quite personal."

"You're in luck. I'm a person. Spill it."

Hoss took in a deep breath. "I killed someone in the fashion industry."

A confession!

"You do have killer looks." Martin rubbed his small hands together merrily. "Tell me everything, Mr. Floor Manager."

Hoss seemed far-away. "When I was a kid, I lived in a rat-infested three-room tenement. My mother passed away in childbirth, and my father didn't stick around. So I lived with my aunt, her four sons, and the peeling walls and floors. Since my uncle was in prison for a crime he didn't commit, to make ends meet, we all worked at a nearby fashion design house."

"You were fashion designers?"

He laughed ironically. "Hardly. My aunt dusted the offices and scrubbed the floors. My cousins and I cleaned the bathrooms. We made enough money for one meal a day, and the meal wasn't exactly fit for a king."

Or a queen.

"Every day after school, I'd watch the designers in their expensive clothing eating exotic lunches and bragging about their trips to Europe, fancy homes, and luxury cars." His handsome face saddened. "When I was ten years old, something snapped inside me. I couldn't take it a moment longer—being subservient and my family having nothing. One day a maintenance worker opened a storage closet full of mink coats, leather jackets, gowns, tuxedos, and other fancy clothes. When he left to answer a page from his supervisor, I wrapped my arms around the biggest bin of clothing I could find and pushed it out the door and down the hallway. Just as I reached the front door of the building, an elderly security guard spotted me and raced toward me. I elbowed him away, and the old man slipped on the wet floor, cracked his head, and lay in a pool of blood. I froze, not knowing what to do. Somebody screamed, "The black kid killed the guard!" After that, it's all a blur—until the judge at the hearing sentenced me to juvenile hall. I was there until I turned sixteen. Then I kept my nose clean, went back to school, got involved in sports and theatre, and won a scholarship to college." His jaw tightened. "But I never lost my distaste for people in the fashion business, except for my new boyfriend who is a fashion major."

"But you had a flashback recently to your childhood days, and you murdered three modeling students and a fashion design professor at your college?"

Hoss snapped out of it. "No! I never hurt anyone again."

Disappointed, Martin told Hoss he'd "make an offer" next week. After Hoss returned to his dorm room, Martin and Ruben (waiting in the dormitory lobby) switched places. However, the elderly gentleman on the sofa looked nothing like Ruben. He was incredibly tall (thanks to shoe lifts) with a pot belly (cushion) and miniscule features (Noah's makeup work). His skin, long hair, beady eyes, pencil-thin mustache, and baggy jumpsuit were all gray.

When Johnny Riley entered the sitting room, the elderly man waved for Johnny to join him on the sofa. Ruben's voice sounded like lightning splitting a tree next to a hot air balloon. "I'd get up if I could. However, at my age it's hit and miss, mostly miss." Once Johnny was seated, Ruben said, "You must be Johnny Riley. I'm Timmy Over the Hill Figure."

The two thin men shook thin hands and Johnny grimaced.

"Thank you for meeting with me." Johnny added,

"When Professor Abbondanza said a fashion designer wanted to interview me for a staff position, I dropped the phone."

My ear is still ringing.

Johnny scratched his bandaged nose with a bandaged finger. "Actually, that wasn't so unusual since I drop my phone all the time." The fashion student opened the portfolio on his lap. "Here are my fashion designs from class."

"I don't care about them."

"You don't?"

Ruben sat like an all-knowing Buddha. "I'll be honest with you, young man. My days are numbered—in two digits. My ex-friend, Ruff Laurie, stole all of my designers. So with the little time I have left, my last wish is to rebuild my company. I am seeking young talent to help steer my ship out of the storm."

"I can steer." Johnny raised his bandaged hands. "I have padding to help me turn the helm."

"I need someone who is tough."

"How's this?" Johnny took off his shoes and socks, exposing bandages on each toe. "An iron fell on them, right before the ironing board hit me. I'm a survivor."

Ruben twirled his thin mustache. When it came off in his hand, he quickly pressed it over his upper lip.

Saved by a hair.

"After what Ruff did to me, I've learned my lesson, young man. This time around I'm hiring loyal designers who will never leave my company."

"I wouldn't be able to leave." Johnny glanced down at his bandaged knees. "I can barely walk."

"And I want people who won't be tempted away by other designers."

Johnny replied, "I wouldn't be tempted. With my new boyfriend, I have all that I want, except for bandages. The stores in Treemeadow are temporarily out of stock."

Ruben said behind gritted teeth, "I want designers who are cutthroat against the competition."

"I can be pretty cutthroat."

Ruben stared at the stick thin eighteen-year-old. "Care to explain?"

Johnny covered his mouth with his bandaged hand. "I probably shouldn't expose myself."

If he did, I'm guessing that would be bandaged too.

Ruben glared at him. "Then I probably shouldn't expose my company to a newbie."

Clearly getting the message, Johnny pulled back his narrow, bandaged shoulders. "I'm a murderer."

Another one? I wondered what Hoss and Johnny had in common.

"I'm listening." Ruben leaned in toward the young man.

Johnny focused forward, as if seeing it all happening in front of him. "My love for design began really early. I remember at seven years old designing a pink, floppy Easter bunny costume for my dog. He looked so adorable in it. I couldn't resist tying him to a tree in front of our house for all the drivers and people walking by to see him. When it came time for my family to sit down for Easter dinner, we ate course after course followed by chocolate replicas of bunnies, eggs, and crosses."

Did Jesus die on a chocolate cross? Hence the term, "Sweet Religion"?

Johnny took in a stilted breath. "That year, Easter Sunday was an unseasonably hot day. My dog, Lucky, must have been overheated out there in that heavy Easter bunny head and body costume. He probably whined and barked for help. But inside the house I couldn't hear him, since my mother played "Here Comes Peter Cotton Tail" and "Were You There When They Crucified My Lord" on the piano. It turned out Lucky wasn't so lucky after all. When I went outside after dinner, I found him dead inside my costume." Johnny shook his head. "I sure hope he was resurrected." Tears filled Johnny's eyes and dribbled down his cheeks. "Thinking back to that story, I fear my love for fashion and design will end with more pain and death."

Ruben perked up. "Why is that? Did you think about losing Lucky, and then murder your fashion classmates and professor?"

"No! But somebody has been killing people in the Fashion Department, and I'm petrified my boyfriend or I might be next!"

Ruben thanked Johnny for interviewing, but he declined hiring him for fear Johnny might do to Ruben's customers what the boy had done to his dog. After Johnny left dejectedly, Martin pranced back into the sitting room, and I squeezed out from behind the bookcase—massaging my stiff back.

"Bravo to me!" Martin did a spin. "I am not only a gifted model and talented actor, but also a snappy sleuth." He nudged my hurting side. "I found out Hoss Packer has murderous tendencies."

"I can relate." Ruben rose and stood next to Martin. "My role-play was not only brilliantly acted and smartly executed, but also uncovered Johnny Riley to be a possible psychopath."

My eyes followed their lobbed barbs like ping pong balls.

Martin sniffed. "I'm guessing your acting was stiff as usual, Ruben."

Ruben replied, "Hm, being stiff. Something I could never accuse *you* of, Martin."

"I certainly have a stiff upper lip in bed each night as you snore in my ear, kick my legs, and chew the ends of my pillow, Ruben! I assume you do those things because you are so much older than me."

"By only four months."

"Four months is the lifespan of a dragonfly."

I turned toward Ruben for a snappy retort. Instead, he

dropped to the floor.

CHAPTER EIGHT

An hour later, I was pacing the waiting room at Treemeadow Hospital. Martin, having just spoken with one daughter, sat on a gray loveseat speaking on his phone to his other daughter. "He's still unconscious. We're expecting him back from the MRI room any minute."

I was shocked at Martin's sense of calm and clear thinking.

He said into the phone, "No, please don't make the trip with the kids yet. I'll keep you posted and let you know when to come." In a saffron bowtie and sweater vest, he returned the phone to his pocket.

I sat next to him, resting a hand on his knee. "How are *you* doing?"

"I'm fine." He glanced at his watch. "This test is taking longer than the others."

Martin becomes hysterical if a fly is in the room. How can he have it so together when his husband of umpteen years is in a coma?

A tall, dark, middle-aged man in a gray suit entered the sitting room. "Mr. Anderson?"

Martin stood. "Yes."

He spoke in an East Indian accent. "I am Dr. Bhasin, the neurologist. Your husband is still unconscious. I spoke with Dr. Kumar, the cardiologist. We believe he had a cerebrovascular accident."

I interjected, "That's a stroke."

"I know what it is," Martin replied.

I asked the doctor, "When do you think Ruben will wake up? Will there be permanent damage?"

"Time will tell."

Martin asked, "May I see him?"

"Of course." Dr. Bhasin added, "Please give us a few minutes to run some quick tests in his room." He was gone.

I placed a hand on Martin's shoulder. "What do you need?"

"Nothing. I'll go in to see Ruben shortly." He sat on an armchair, staring out the window.

Not knowing what else to do, I stepped out into the hallway and phoned Noah with an update on Ruben, hoping I wouldn't be visiting Noah in the hospital any time soon. From my peripheral vision, I spotted Shayla hurrying toward the sitting room and running to Martin. The moment he saw her, Martin leapt from his seat, collapsed into her arms, and wept bitterly. She patted his small back and rocked him back and forth.

A few minutes later, Shayla and I stood in the hallway outside of Ruben's room. Tubes and wires connected him to various machines that beeped, flashed, and grinded. Martin sat on a gray chair at his husband's bedside. Taking Ruben's hand, he said, "My life didn't really begin until I met you. I was alive, but not living, just existing, lonely, afraid, and without purpose. Overlooked by others for being short, skinny, gay, and ordinary. I entered the classroom on the first day of dramatic literature class. As in all my other college freshman classes, I wasn't surprised when no other student made eye contact with me. But that day was different. There you sat, looking handsome, regal, and smart. You looked at me and smiled. When I sat next to you, it was as if the part of me that had been missing my entire life was suddenly found." Martin smiled. "The professor must have hated us, as we talked through his entire lecture, sharing our childhoods, adolescences, likes, dislikes, hopes, fears, and goals for the future. I knew by the end of that class we were soulmates. And I was right. School, more school, careers, children, grandchildren, and show after show after show — on stage and off." Martin kissed his hand. "We started this long, winding, bumpy, glorious journey together. And I can't continue walking without you by my side: to be honest with me when I stumble, help navigate my next steps, catch me when I fall, and smooth the road ahead of us — laughing and loving all the way. Don't leave me alone, trying to feel my way in the dark without you. Stay on the road — by my side. Hold my hand, my dear love, and guide me through the last leg of the race." Martin wept into Ruben's chest.

"You're wetting the sheets, Martin, and not in a good way."

Martin threw his arms around his husband's shoulders. "Thank you for coming back to me." He smiled at Ruben's pale face. "I thought I might be a handsome, sexy, mysterious widower."

"No chance of *that* happening."

"You mean you're going to get well?"

"That too."

They shared a long embrace. So did Shayla and I before I summoned the doctor, who thankfully offered a promising prediction of Ruben's full recovery.

By the time I left the hospital and drove home, the sky enveloped me in an appropriately pink ribbon that opened to a charcoal sky. After entering our kitchen, I thankfully gobbled down the dinner Noah had left for me on the counter. Then I hurried up the flared oak staircase. Hearing voices from Taavi's room, I made my way down the hall and sat on my side of the sleigh bed. Sitting opposite me, Noah asked, "How's Ruben?"

"Awake and bantering with Martin." I breathed a sigh of relief. "The doctor's prognosis was very positive."

"Thank goodness." Noah kissed my cheek.

Under the sheet, Taavi gazed up at us wide-eyed.

I asked, "What's wrong?"

"Nothing."

Though a good actor, I saw through Taavi's charade. "What's going on?"

Taavi bit his lip.

Noah offered, "Taavi's afraid that what happened to Ruben might happen to you or me someday."

Noah and I exchanged a knowing glance.

"Is that what you're worried about?" I asked.

Taavi nodded, blinking back tears.

I ran my hand along his cheek. "Taavi, no matter what challenges any of us encounter, the three of will always be connected, as a family."

He leaned up on one elbow. "But what if you or Dad gets sick, and you pass away?"

Mustering all of his acting skills, Noah said, "We're *all* going to pass away someday, hopefully not for a long time, but we'll still be together."

Taavi asked, "Do you mean in the spirit world?"

"Sure," I replied.

Not relenting, Taavi asked, "But how do we know the spirit world really exists?"

"It exists in our memories, thoughts, and love." Noah kissed his forehead. "Your pop and I love you, and we always will. Nothing can ever change that. No matter what happens to any of us. Okay?"

"Okay." Taavi gazed out the window at the half moon.

"What is it now?" I rested him onto his back.

"Pop, I think I have an idea about who killed Shane, Julio, Cosmo, Lila, and Tyler Greenway."

Noah and I shared a quick look. I asked, "Want to tell us about it?"

Taavi shook his head. "It's just a crazy idea. It can't be right." His light snore followed.

I tucked the sheet under his chin, stood, shut the light, and walked with Noah to our bedroom.

As we changed into our T-shirts and boxers, Noah said, "Taavi is justifiably upset about Ruben, and even more worried about the murders."

"I know."

We met at the foot of the bed. Noah rested a hand on my cheek. "Nicky, whatever the blood tests results show, I want you to know that I wouldn't have traded a minute of my life with you and Taavi. And there's nobody happier than me."

"I love you so much."

My husband and I shared a long embrace. When I reached out to check his throat glands, Noah pulled away, reached into the drawer under my bed, and offered my laptop. "Stop worrying about me. It's time to solve the case, Nicky."

Once Noah and I were snug in our fourposter, I rested the laptop on my knees. "You want to help?"

Like his son before him, Noah responded with a gentle snore. I opened a new file on my computer. Glad to have something to take my mind off Noah's test results, I typed.

The Case of the Toxic Runway

Victims: Shane Buff (modeling student), Julio Bonero (modeling student), Cosmo Capra (modeling student), Lila Hekekia (fashion design student), Tyler Greenway (Associate Professor of Fashion Design).

Suspects and Motives: Ulla Ultimate, designer and visiting professor (wasn't happy about her son's flirting with Shane Buff and Julio Bonero, wanted overweight Cosmo Capra out of her show, angry Lila Hekekia tried to close down Ulla's show, outraged that Tyler Greenway impregnated and dumped her in college claiming she stole his designs); Cory Ultimate, theatre set design student and model (dumped by Shane Buff, rejected by Julio Bonero and Cosmo Capra, probably

*angry Lila Hekekia tried to close down Ulla's show,
enraged at Tyler Greenway for rejecting him as his son);
Miles Jeffrey, Ulla Ultimate's assistant and model
(could have been jealous of Cory's tryst with Shane Buff,
might have wanted Julio Bonero out of the picture to
date Cory himself, could have wanted Cosmo Capra
gone to take his modeling spot in the show, upset Lila
Hekekia tried to close down his boss's show and take the
slot for herself, angered by Tyler Greenway's rejection
of Cory); Johnny Riley, fashion design student (jealous
of Shane Buff's and Julio Bonero's attention to Hoss
Packer, probably unhappy Lila Hekekia tried to close
down Ulla's show, has a violent history); Hoss Packer,
theatre stage managing student (bothered by Shane
Buff's and Julio Bonero's come-ons, probably unhappy
Lila Hekekia tried to close down the show, has a violent
history).*

I stared blankly at the screen. *What am I missing?* As I
closed the laptop and placed it on my night table, I thought
about the woman in white. *Who is she? Why is she in the
fashion theatre at night? Did she know Shane, Julio, Cosmo, Lila,
and Tyler?* Visions of her flowing blonde hair and gorgeous
ivory gown flooded my consciousness, as I drifted off to
sleep.

CHAPTER NINE

The next day, I woke, showered, put on my body cream, and ate breakfast (chard broccoli manchego cheese crepes with pear guava elderberry smoothies and vitamins) with Noah and Taavi at the nook. After Taavi had gone upstairs to his room, Noah's phone rang. It slipped out of his hands. After retrieving it from the kitchen floor, he looked at the screen and said, "Dr. Jeff." Noah and I quickly sat holding hands at the breakfast nook with the phone between us on speaker.

Dr. Jeff's hoarse voice projected through the phone. "Noah, how are you feeling?"

"The lymph nodes have gone down a bit." Noah's voice quivered. "Are the test results in?"

"Most of them." Dr. Jeff exhaled deeply. "Only one thing's come up so far."

I squeezed Noah's sweaty hand.

"Markers suggest it could be an allergic reaction. Have you eaten nuts lately?"

"No." Noah scratched his head.

"Have you used a new soap, deodorant, or other topical product?"

Noah and I gasped. I shouted first, "My new skin cream. Noah used it before having the reaction!"

Dr. Jeff replied, "Stop using it."

"I have," Noah said.

"That's probably why your glands have gone down a bit. If it's the skin cream, and I think it is, you should be back to normal soon."

I couldn't stop the tears from flowing down my cheeks. Noah's mixed with mine as we shared a hug.

Dr. Jeff said, "Call me in two days."

Noah cleared his throat. "I will, Dr. Jeff. Thank you."

"My pleasure. You two boys stay out of trouble now." He added, "But solve the murder mystery fast."

"We will!" Noah and I said in unison.

After literally jumping for joy in each other's arms, Noah and I celebrated with a grape juice toast—and the disposal of my anti-aging skin cream. Back in the kitchen with my arms around the man of my heart, I said, "Nothing will ever take you away from me."

"I'm yours forever."

We shared a long kiss as I silently thanked the gods.

Then remembering our opening night, Noah and I cleaned up the kitchen, visited Ruben in the hospital, had lunch there with Martin, came home for a rest and dinner, and then squeezed into our tuxedos.

After Noah drove Taavi and me to campus faster than a Republican politician denying having had private meetings with Russian spies, we beelined it for the fashion theatre. I checked in with Hoss Packer at the lighting booth (who was going over his cues), Ulla in the house (taking a tranquilizer), Johnny Riley in the sewing room (bandaging his navel), and finally the five models in the dressing room (sucking in their stomachs and puffing out their chests).

I put a reassuring arm around Martin's narrow shoulders. "How's Ruben doing?"

Martin grinned like a school kid at a bomb scare. "If all continues to go well, the doctor said he can come home in a few days—good as new! It will be like taking up with a new man!"

"I'm happy for you—both."

Martin giggled. "So am I!"

Then turning to the other side of the dressing room, I

said, "Have a good show, guys!"

Cory Ultimate and Miles Jeffrey gazed into each other's eyes lovingly. "We will."

They talk in unison too!

They shared a long kiss.

I headed down the runway, out the inside door, and to the center of the lobby, where I met up again with Noah and Taavi.

My thoughtful husband asked, "How's Martin?"

"In the pink." (*pun intended*) "Just like you."

We shared a congratulatory hug.

Oblivious, Taavi texted Tia.

Then Noah asked me, "And Miles and Cory?"

"Looks like Miles won't be interviewing possible husbands for Cory any longer—now that Miles found someone for Cory: Miles."

"Juicy."

"So was their kiss in the dressing room."

Detective Manuello barreled over to me like a shark spotting an overweight surfer. "This is it, Nicky. You promised to solve the case by the curtain call."

"And he will." Noah patted my shoulder.

"I will?"

Manuello growled.

"Yes, I will. Hang tight, Manuello." I patted the rolls of fat hanging over his belt. "If that's possible."

Manuello adjusted his wrinkled dark suit jacket over his stomach. "Just catch the murderer, Nicky. Unless you want to feel my belt against your backstage."

"Manuello, please, control your fantasies! My husband and child are present!"

He groaned and walked away.

Noah giggled. Taavi continued texting.

The audience members started to arrive in flurries of spring suits, dresses, and gowns. Shayla Johnson appeared in a tangerine satin dress. I met her near the outside double doors into the lobby. Pressing a loose strand of hair back inside the dark bun at her neck, she asked, "Where's the lord and master?"

'Master' being the operative word. "Martin's backstage changing into his black leather outfit for the opening."

"Ruben sends his love, wishing he could be here. Not!" She laughed wildly.

I smiled. "Enjoy the show, Shayla."

"I always do."

"Mr. Abbondanza! Mr. Oliver!" Tia, in a red, white, and blue striped dress, ushered her parents toward us. They wore a drab suit and fire-engine red muumuu respectively.

"Hello, Tedescos. Thank you for coming," I said.

"We wouldn't miss it for the world." Helen Tedesco gawked at Noah like a priest finding an altar boy wading in holy water. "And look at that tuxedo!" Helen Tedesco giggle snorted, and her red curls bobbed around her face like miniature buoys in a storm. "Noah, you look good enough to eat!"

"Thank you."

I cleared my throat.

"Next to Nicky on a wedding cake!"

Tia blushed. "Mom."

"What? The gays can get married now too."

Just like real people.

Helen added, "And aren't you both dapper. Now I see where Taavi gets his good looks. Which one of you impregnated a Hawaiian girl? Or did you do it in a test tube while looking at a men's magazine?"

Tia whispered in her mother's ear, "Taavi was adopted."

"Then I'd love to meet Taavi's birth father too!" Helen laughed again.

"Hello, Nicky and Noah." Bill Tedesco extended a long hand and shook ours. "Any more trouble from that religious fanatic you told us about? Did you fight for what's yours and put the nutcase in her place?"

Helen slapped his shoulder. "Don't you read the news, Bill? Lila Kekekia was murdered."

Bill sighed. "I guess if you wait long enough, anybody who annoys you in Treemeadow will be murdered." He grinned. "One of the bonuses of living here."

Tia beamed at Taavi. "You look so cool, Taavi."

"You look really cool too, Tia."

They grabbed their phones and began texting each other.

I spotted the local reporter and her camera operator. Ulla Ultimate, clad in a black leather gown and necklace, stood before the camera, adjusting her platinum wig. I excused myself and raced over.

The young, thin reporter sported a skintight cerise mini dress with more makeup on her face than a Geisha girl. "Tell us about your new fashion line, Ulla."

Ulla's cheek implants wobbled, as she replied, "My new men's line is modern, sleek, chic, comfortable, wearable, and sexy."

The reporter crinkled her surgically altered nose. "Why pick Treemeadow College as the launching pad for it?"

"My son is a student here."

The journalist sniffed. "Yes, Cory Ultimate. Isn't he a homosexual?"

"Last time I checked," Ulla replied.

"Is the rumor true that you are slapping the face of everyone who believes in family values by having your personal assistant seek a so-called 'husband' for Cory?"

Ulla's eyes widened like violets in springtime. "Yes, among Miles' other duties."

Like dating Cory himself.

"What do you have to say to your critics who believe your designs are nothing more than a fulfillment of the homosexual fantasy?"

"*My* fantasies are certainly fulfilled." I stood next to Ulla. "But then again my husband's in the show."

The reporter asked, "Nicky Abbondanza, as the director of the Ulla Ultimate Fashion Show, isn't this entire evening simply part of the homosexual agenda?"

"It is most definitely part of *this* homosexual's agenda." I offered my best smile to the camera. "But only if the audience members stand up, cheer, and cry, 'Director! Director!' at the end of the show."

Ulla made her way over to some visiting fashion dignitaries.

The reporter's tight face aimed in my direction. "Nicky, what do you say to the charges of evangelicals everywhere that fashion student Lila Hekekia was murdered as a Christian martyr for daring to believe in God and family."

"I'd say, 'Where are the lions and dungeons when you need them?'"

Her eyes narrowed. "As a shameless homosexual—"

"I have to disagree with you there. I can behave pretty shamefully."

"—and an amateur sleuth, what do you have to say to the decent citizens of Treemeadow who, after five murders, are justifiably frightened to leave their homes?"

"I'd tell them to put their faith in me. I, Nicky Abbondanza, armchair detective, will solve this case by the end of the night." *I hope.*

She turned to the camera. "You heard it here, folks. The homosexual lobby would like you to believe their murders will finally end this evening. Fake news from Professor Nicky Abbondanza of the educational elite? It sure sounds like it to me."

"Ahhhh!"

"Ahhhh!"

I followed the screams to Mama and Papa in a corner

of the lobby with Noah and Taavi. After suffocating hugs and loud kisses were exchanged, Papa rubbed his bald head. "How are our three boys!"

"Fine, Papa," I replied.

Noah rubbed his ear. "Thank you for making the long trip from Kansas."

Papa lit up like a birthday cake. "We wouldn't miss it for all the Italian pastries in my bakery."

Taavi asked, "Did you bring any with you, Grandpapa?"

Papa reached into his dark suit jacket pocket. "Look what I just found: a cannoli!"

I stepped between them. "Taavi's a model now. Runway first. Dessert later."

Papa winked at Taavi. "Meet you in your bedroom when we get back to the house."

Taavi nodded conspiratorially.

Always the gracious host, Noah said, "The guest room is ready for you, Mama and Papa."

Papa replied, "Good. After the show, we'll unload the rest of the pastries from the car into that nice bureau in there."

Thankfully we don't have mice – yet.

Mama hollered, "Look at my grandson. How you've grown!" She wrenched him into her chest. "We can't wait to see you in another show!"

"I can't wait for you to see me in another show too." Taavi kissed her cheek. "Grandmama, the way you and Grandpapa always wear black clothes, you could be in our fashion show."

Mama spun around in her matronly black dress. "Who knew we were fashion plates, Papa?"

"*I* did." He poked her, and they shared a laugh. "Those skinny models could use a good dose of our pastry!"

"Come on, Papa, let's go into the theatre and walk down the runway before the show starts." Mama took

Papa's hand.

Papa leaned into me. "Have you solved the murder mystery yet?"

I gasped. "You heard about the murders all the way in Kansas?"

"No. But there's always a murder to solve whenever *you're* around, Nicky."

Mama tugged at my arm. "I know people in the casino business. Tell me if you need help wiping anyone out. Pun intended."

They disappeared inside the theatre.

An iPhone appeared followed by Noah's mother. "Judy from Wisconsin said you look more handsome than her nephew—when he was laid out in his casket!"

"How's my guys!" Noah's dad laughed merrily.

Noah, Taavi, and I embraced Mom and Dad.

"I'm really glad you're both here." Noah seemed to really mean it.

"Where else would we be on opening night?" Mom welcomed Noah's hug.

Taavi asked, "Thank you for coming to see me, Grandma and Grandpa. Did you bring any cheese?"

"We sure did." Like a magician, Dad produced a round of cheese from his inside jacket pocket.

Taavi gave him the hang loose sign.

Noah cleared his throat. "Taavi has a show to do."

Dad winked at Taavi. "We'll save this for a late-night snack back at the house."

Noah thought fast. "The attic room is ready for you, Mom and Dad."

"Wonderful!" Mom and Dad smiled as if planning to stay at Buckingham Palace.

Taavi said, "When we get home, over cheese and crackers, you can tell me how much you liked me in the show."

Mom kissed Taavi, leaving peach lips all over his face.

"I'm so proud of you." She patted the side of her gray blonde hair. "When I was younger, *I* had aspirations to be a model."

Noah took out his handkerchief and wiped the lipstick off Taavi's face. "I remember you setting up my scout tent and cot in the living room to use as your practice runway, Mom."

"Sadly, my dreams never left the living room." Mom's blue eyes danced. "Perhaps tonight will be my big break?"

"The show is all set, Mom."

I turned to Noah. "I didn't know you were a scout."

He blushed. "It was a long time ago."

Dad scratched himself, clearly uncomfortable in his dark suit. "Yeah, Noah was a scout. He spent many nights outside camping."

No pun intended.

Mom added, "But Noah was too embarrassed to do wee-wee in front of the other boys. So, when they all headed for the woods to do their business, Noah went so far into the woods he got poison ivy all over his little johnboy. It was red and itchy for a week!"

I rested an arm around Noah. "Noah never told me about his red and itchy johnboy."

His face turned green.

Dad glanced at his watch. "Guys, how long is the show?"

"Under two hours with the intermission," I replied. *And then I have to name the murderer!*

"That's okay." Dad lifted the smart phone from his inside shirt pocket. "I can watch my movies during the show — on this."

Noah asked, "What movies do you want to watch?"

Dad scratched his protruding stomach. "*The Devil Wears Prada* and *Zoolander* are on."

Mom raised her iPhone and took a picture of Noah, Taavi, and me. After breezing over her keypad, she said,

"Judy thinks you are an adorable family. She wishes Tommy, Timmy, and Dung would dress up too."

I bit. "How are your neighbor's son and his family?"

Mom rested her arms on the bosom of her peach dress. "Not so good, I'm afraid. Poor little Dung missed her homeland in Vietnam. So Tommy and Timmy took her to see a local touring production of *Miss Saigon*. They had front row seats."

"That must have set Jack back a pretty penny."

Ignoring Dad, Mom said, "Little Dung loved the show so much she raced onto the stage, and Dung got all over the helicopter. After the show, Tommy and Timmy brought the little girl to the stage door to apologize to the actors. Wouldn't you know, Dung flew at the actors and covered them from head to toe."

Dad whispered in my ear, "Have you solved the case yet?"

My jaw dropped. "How do you know I'm working on a case?"

"You're always working on a case."

Mom waved my question away. "It seems more people have been killed in Treemeadow than in World War II." She pinched my cheek. "But I know my brilliant son-in-law will solve the case again."

"With my help," Noah said.

"And mine," Taavi added.

I rested a hand on each of their shoulders. "Noah and Taavi need to dress for the opening number and get warmed up."

"Yeah, you don't want to be stiff Noah — until later tonight with Nicky." Dad laughed uproariously.

The lights flashed in the lobby.

Blushing, Noah thankfully took the cue. "Enjoy the show, Mom and Dad. Taavi, come with me."

The four of them disappeared. When the lobby was empty, I entered the theatre and took my seat in the last row. I scanned the room full of photographers, fashion designers, clothing buyers, and reviewers. Holding my breath, I watched as the house lights went out and the stage lights came on—*the correct color*. I didn't breathe until the end of the opening number. The lighting and music cues were perfect. The choreography was clean and well executed. Despite Ruben's health scare, Martin was bouncy and bold. Noah, with reignited vitality, had the audience in the palm of his hand—or a bit lower. Cory and Miles were seductive and alluring—especially to each other. Taavi, of course, stole the show with his winks to the audience and stage charisma. During the strong applause after the activewear section, I settled into my chair as the rest of the first half (clubwear, nightwear, casualwear) went along equally well. Sitting in the darkened theatre, I replayed in my mind everything that had happened over the last week. Using my insights as a theatre director, I thought about each suspect as a character, trying to uncover their actions, objectives, motivations, and the obstacles in the way of them achieving their goals. I saw every facial expression, and I heard every bit of dialogue— including each pause. I leapt from my seat. Thankfully it was intermission. I nodded my appreciation amidst shouts of praise and applause as the audience headed to the lobby. Then I raced up the runway and into the sewing room, where I came nose to bandaged nose with Johnny Riley. "Johnny, I figured it out, and it's about time we have a talk."

Chapter Ten

Johnny pretended not to understand. "I peeked out at the runway from backstage. The show looked terrific. And I checked all the wardrobe in the dressing room, and there's nothing in need of repair."

"I think you know what I'm talking about."

His narrow shoulders slumped, and he sat on the edge of his sewing table. "How did you figure it out?"

"You said you were working at the dye bin, which can be used for bleaching, and at the steamer — neither of which are needed for Ulla Ultimate's all black leather outfits. And you mentioned wanting to be a model."

He sighed. "I hope you won't tell anyone."

"I'm guessing Hoss knows. That's why you behaved so oddly around him at first."

He nodded. "Hoss is turned on by it, but others may mock me. So Hoss promised to keep my secret. Will you do the same, Professor?"

"Yes." I gazed at his bandaged face. "But *you* need to tell everyone, Johnny."

He rose and turned his back to me. "I don't know if I can do that, Professor."

I grasped his shoulders and moved him around to face me. "Johnny, you have an incredible talent. It needs to be shared."

He laughed. "Dressing up in drag and prancing around the runway after everyone leaves isn't a talent."

"Sure it is! As that famous drag model said, 'we all

dress in drag every day when we decide what clothes to wear.' And your clothes, the way you look, your persona on the runway is magical, ephemeral, and beautiful."

Johnny's face lit up like a ceramic village. "Do you really think so, Professor?"

"I know so." Snapping my fingers, I added, "Where's your dress and wig?"

Johnny opened a cabinet and held up the blonde wig and white gown.

"As director, I've decided to add a special closing to the show. After the finale and curtain call, I'd like you to walk down the runway and welcome Ulla Ultimate to the stage for her bow."

"Are you serious?"

"As serious as a Republican president at the shredder after a meeting with Russian money launderers." I smiled with encouragement. "Johnny, take off those bandages. Get into your outfit. And don't be ashamed of your inner light. Hold the candle high and let it shine."

"Thank you, Professor." He gazed at the wig and gown, grinning.

"And thank you for calling the EMT when I fell in the theatre house."

Johnny didn't answer, lost in visions of his upcoming public debut as the woman in the white.

I hurried back to the house and took my seat. The second act flew by with the models perfectly showcasing Ulla's bathing suits, kinky attire, and formalwear. During the finale number, I watched Cory Ultimate and thought about how a parent's words can mold a child—sometimes for the worse. As the song goes, "Children Will Listen." *That's it! I think I know the identity of the mass murderer! But can it be? I need to find out.* I blurted aloud, "And I need to protect Noah and Taavi backstage!"

The show ended to tumultuous applause. The models reentered for their bows to cheers of "Bravo!" Johnny, or rather the woman in white, entered the runway to an astonished but captivated hush and then to jubilant cheers. When Ulla Ultimate mounted the steps for a bow, the crowd went wild. Then the models returned to the dressing room to change, and the audience flooded Ulla Ultimate with praises. I bobbed and weaved through their congratulatory comments and slaps on the back as I mounted the runway and ran backstage. When I arrived at the dressing room door, a broomstick knocked me in the head. I wobbled to gain my balance, as a hand yanked me into the sewing shop, locked the door behind us, and then pushed me into the open steamer. With my head sticking out of the top, I felt the sides of the steamer begin to close in on me. Struggling frantically, I was unable to move. My captor pressed another button and hot steam began to surround me.

"I heard what you said out there about 'protecting Noah and Taavi.' When I saw the look on your face, I knew you had figured it out. Very uncool. So I ran backstage before you, needing to wipe you out, before you wiped out me." Tia Tedesco stood hovering over me with a maniacal look on her young face. "'Strike down your enemy before he strikes you down.' Just as my parents always taught me."

I tried to scream but my throat quickly filled with steam. My skin burned, and I became lightheaded.

"Johnny Riley didn't know I was watching him steam that cool white gown. It took three minutes. I'm guessing you'll be done in about the same time." She guffawed. "Wrinkle free, out of my hair, and as my mom says: 'dead as a moth in a vat of vinegar.'"

Think clearly. Keep her talking until Noah finds me. I took in a deep breath and my lungs filled with steam. Somehow I managed to gasp out, "Your parents will be looking for you."

She cackled. "I told them I was visiting with Taavi

backstage. Then I texted Taavi to meet me in a few minutes in the alley behind the dressing room—where I silenced Shane Buff." Tia flipped her dark hair behind her shoulders. "My parents? Is that how you figured it out, Mr. Abbondanza?"

I nodded.

"Like I said, my dad's my hero. You heard his totally cool words of wisdom at your house that night: 'take what you want,' 'squash the competition,' 'kids must obey their parents.' My mom was pretty cool too with her advice to: 'fight for your man and always stand by him.' I've listened to those totally cool things ever since I can remember, and I totally live by them. That night after *you* had heard my parents' cool philosophies, I wondered if you might figure out what I'd done."

Don't black out. Keep alert. I rasped out through the steam, "You heard Shane Buff advise Taavi to play the field and enjoy life to the fullest."

Her face contorted into a rage. "So when Shane was out in the alley, I hit him with the mannequin from the sewing room. I wouldn't let that stiff come between Taavi and me. Taavi is totally cool, and he's totally mine!"

I wish I had some cool air. I feel like I've got the worst sunburn of my life! "You were there when Julio Bonero told Taavi to dedicate his life to his career and never believe anyone loves him."

"So I used the sheering scissors to cut those words out of Julio's big mouth." She sniggered. "Julio met his fate in this very room. And Taavi still believes I love him, which I do!"

Where's Noah? I choked out, "You suffocated Cosmo Capra and then sewed his lips together because he fed Taavi so many sweets."

"Taavi deserves to have a totally cool career. That won't happen if Taavi doesn't stay hot—and fit." She stared maniacally. "I'll always make sure of that."

Feeling as if I'd stayed in the steam room overnight, I became weak and disoriented. Looking at three Tias in front of me, I rasped out, "Lila Hekekia asked Taavi to hurry up and grow so she can marry him."

"So I hit that psycho Jesus freak with a Fresnel until she saw the light." Tia laughed hysterically at her own joke. Then she instantly scowled in a fury. "Nobody is marrying Taavi—but me!"

I felt my head dropping. "You heard Tyler Greenway tell Taavi never to get serious with a woman."

"Which made me get serious with Tyler Greenway. When he wasn't looking, I poured Johnny Riley's bleach into Greenway's flask." Her eyes were wild and on fire. "Greenway may have fled from Ulla Ultimate, but Taavi will strut down the aisle like a runway with me by his side at our totally cool wedding!" She walked toward me. "Now I just have to watch you steam like rice, and I'm free to follow my parents' advice and be with the coolest guy in the world—forever. So, Mr. Abbondanza, it looks like you're just about cooked."

The room spun around me and began to dim.

Suddenly, the door opened with a bang. Three Noahs ran toward me as three Manuellos handcuffed Tia. Taavi confronted her. "Tia, how could you do this?"

I heard the echoes of Tias cries as two officers led her out of the sewing room. "I did it for you, Taavi. So we could have a totally cool life together. I needed to fight for what's mine. And you're mine, Taavi. You always will be. I'll never stop fighting for you. Text me!"

Manuello phoned for the paramedics.

Noah shut off the steamer and lifted me to freedom. I rested weakly against his chest and whispered, "You're my savior."

"And you're mine." As I started to fade off, Noah shouted, "Stay with me, Nicky."

"You're the love of my life, Noah."

"I'll always love you, Nicky."

Taavi appeared in front of me. "Pop, when I told you and Dad in my bedroom I had a theory about the murders, I wondered about Tia's neediness. But I just couldn't believe she would murder anyone."

Noah added, "After the show when Tia didn't meet Taavi in the alley as planned, he came to me. We found the sewing room door locked. Since you weren't out front milking the audience's praises, Taavi figured it all out."

I reached for his hand. "You're a fine sleuth, son." *I just wish you had figured it out a few minutes sooner.*

The emergency medical team arrived with a stretcher and oxygen. I glanced up at them and the room turned to darkness.

EPILOGUE

Two weeks later, Noah, Taavi, and I were back in our tuxedos at Ulla Ultimate's Treemeadow Hotel suite. The gracious host, in a black leather gown and silver spiked necklace, flitted from guest to guest in the large sitting room encased with white walls embroidered with gold molding. Standing next to me at the buffet table in the center of the room, Manuello, in his dark wrinkled suit, rammed a Thai chicken meatball into his mouth. "Well, Nicky, it looks like you solved another case." He slapped my back.

"Ow!"

Noah explained, "His skin is still tender from being trapped in that steamer."

Taavi added, "But Pop's new anti-aging skin cream saved him." He grinned. "So did I."

I kissed my husband and son.

"I'm glad the cream was good for something." Noah smiled, back to full health.

I hugged my husband into my chest.

"Anti-aging cream?" Manuello ran a hand through his graying hair. "Why do homosexuals fear aging so much?"

"Is that part of your comedy act?"

Manuello glared at me. "I know you're teasing me, Nicky."

"Actually, I'm not." I explained, "I've booked you into my friend's nightclub in Key West. The gay crowd on the pier is really looking forward to 'The Deviant Detective's

Standup Act.'"

"You didn't!" He advanced on me.

I smiled. "No, I didn't, Manuello. But I can if you'd like."

"I don't like." He grabbed a potato stuffed with tiny scallops, avocado, and goat cheese. "I plan to remain a detective in Treemeadow for many years to come."

"And *that's* why we fear aging so much." I patted his shoulder. "It's been lovely, as usual, chatting with you, but since this is a party, it's time for me to mingle."

"Is that a gay thing?" he asked.

"Yes, especially at the baths. Put that in your act."

"There is no act!"

"Keep saying that and maybe you'll believe it." I excused myself and walked past the white and gold fireplace mantel to Martin and Ruben sitting on a white and gold loveseat. "How's the patient?"

Martin adjusted his apricot-colored bowtie and sweater vest. "I'm relieved the stroke left no permanent damage, and Ruben's physical therapy is going so well!"

Ruben straightened the pleat of his apricot leisure suit. "Except for this annoying little pain."

Martin asked, "Is your leg still bothering you, Ruben?"

"No, Martin."

"Then which little pain were you…?"

They burst out laughing and fell into each other's arms.

I continued over to the sofa and joined Johnny Riley and Hoss Packer, dressed in matching red suits. "You two young gents look festive."

"And we feel festive too." Hoss grinned.

Johnny clasped his bandaged hands at his bandaged chest. "Professor, I'm floating on air."

Like a ghost.

"I still can't believe that agent saw me in Ulla's runway show and offered me a job in a drag show in Las Vegas!"

"You'll be wonderful, Johnny," I replied, meaning it.

"So will Hoss." Johnny explained, "I got him an interview with the director."

"It went really well." Hoss smiled. "I'll be stage managing the show!"

Let's hope the show takes place in the dark. "Congratulations to you both." I grinned. "I hear a lot of people get married in Las Vegas." Sounding like Martin, I asked, "Is that in the cards (*pun intended*) for you two?"

Hoss leaned over, and his muscles practically burst out of his tuxedo. "As a matter of fact, Professor, we're engaged!"

They displayed their rings.

"I'm happy for you. At the ceremony, say hi to Elvis for me."

"May I have everyone's attention?" At the front of the room, Ulla Ultimate stood beside Cory Ultimate and Miles Jeffrey — both looking dashing in white tuxedos. "I was incredibly happy when my son and I reconciled our differences."

Cory smiled merrily.

"But now I'm even more elated. While I may be losing an assistant, I'm gaining another son. Love and the best wishes to you both on your engagement."

Cory and Miles kissed each of her cheeks. Then they fell into a long embrace.

Ulla added, "And we hope to see you all at the wedding!"

I made my way over to them. "Congratulations to the grooms."

"Thank you, Professor." Cory took Miles' hand. "We're both looking forward to the wedding, and to our careers as models."

"I'm proud of what I started."

Miles winked at me. "And we're proud to pick up the ball and run with it. Right into each other's arms."

They kissed again.

Taking Ulla's arm, I ushered her to a corner of the room. "Congratulations on your hit fashion show, and also for being the mother of the groom."

She sighed. "I want whatever makes Cory happy. So, I'm willing to give up a good assistant like Miles."

"But that was the plan all along. Wasn't it, Ulla?"

"What do you mean?"

"When you interviewed for assistants, you were really seeking a husband for Cory. After you selected Miles, you couldn't tell Cory about it for fear he'd run away from any man you picked for him. So you gave Miles the task of interviewing men for Cory, hoping Miles and Cory would fall in love. And they did—according to *your* plan."

She smiled like the Cheshire cat. "Let's keep that little secret under our black leather caps, hmm Nicky?"

"I aim to please, Mistress."

We shared a laugh. Hearing my stomach growl, I headed back to the buffet table. After filling my plate with gourmet food, I glanced down at Taavi's empty dish. "Not hungry?"

"I'm still bummed out about Tia."

Noah rested a hand on his shoulder. "Tia's parents phoned. They've been visiting her in juvenile prison and going to family counseling."

Taavi grimaced. "How could I not have known what Tia was up to?"

Noah squeezed his shoulder. "You had no way of reading Tia's mind."

"But I fell for a murderer! What kind of loser am I?"

I took pity on Taavi's pity party. "On the bright side, you saved your dad and me from the daughter-in-law from Hell."

Taavi sulked. "The next time I fall for a girl, she's going to be just like me."

"Not a murderer?" Noah asked.

"In show business, and an amateur sleuth."

"Thank the mystery gods. And *all* the gods." I put my arms around my husband and son. "Here's to us being together, good health, crime-solving, and the best art there is — the art of show!"

★

ABOUT THE AUTHOR

Bestselling author JOE COSENTINO was voted Favorite LGBT Mystery, Humorous, and Contemporary Author of the Year by the readers of Divine Magazine for *Drama Queen*. He also wrote the other novels in the Nicky and Noah mystery series: *Drama Muscle, Drama Cruise, Drama Luau, Drama Detective, Drama Fraternity, Drama Castle, Drama Dance, Drama Faerie, Drama Runway*; the Dreamspinner Press novellas: *In My Heart/An Infatuation & A Shooting Star*, the Bobby and Paolo Holiday Stories: *A Home for the Holidays/The Perfect Gift/The First Noel*, Tales from Fairyland: *The Naked Prince and Other Tales from Fairyland/Holiday Tales from Fairyland*; the Cozzi Cove series: *Cozzi Cove: Bouncing Back, Cozzi Cove: Moving Forward, Cozzi Cove: Stepping Out, Cozzi Cove: New Beginnings, Cozzi Cove: Happy Endings* (NineStar Press); and the Jana Lane mysteries: *Paper Doll, Porcelain Doll, Satin Doll, China Doll, Rag Doll* (The Wild Rose Press). He has appeared in principal acting roles in film, television, and theatre, opposite stars such as Bruce Willis, Rosie O'Donnell, Nathan Lane, Holland Taylor, and Jason Robards. Joe is currently Chair of the Department/Professor at a college in upstate New York and is happily married. Joe was voted 2nd Place Favorite LGBT Author of the Year in Divine Magazine's Readers' Choice Awards, and his books have received numerous Favorite Book of the Month Awards and Rainbow Award Honorable Mentions.

Connect with this author on social media

Web site: http://www.JoeCosentino.weebly.com
Facebook: http://www.facebook.com/JoeCosentinoauthor
Twitter: https://twitter.com/JoeCosen
Amazon: http://Author.to/JoeCosentino
Goodreads: https://www.goodreads.com/author/show/ 4071647.Joe_Cosentino

And don't miss any of the
Nicky and Noah mysteries
by Joe Cosentino

DRAMA QUEEN

It could be curtains for college theatre professor Nicky Abbondanza. With dead bodies popping up all over campus, Nicky must use his drama skills to figure out who is playing the role of murderer before it is lights out for Nicky and his colleagues. Complicating matters is Nicky's huge crush on Noah Oliver, a gorgeous assistant professor in his department, who may or may not be involved with Nicky's cocky graduate assistant and is also the top suspect for the murders! You will be applauding and shouting Bravo for Joe Cosentino's fast-paced, side-splittingly funny, edge-of-your-seat, delightfully entertaining novel. Curtain up!

Winner of *Divine Magazine*'s Readers' Poll Awards as Favorite LGBT Mystery, Crime, Humorous, and Contemporary novel of 2015!

DRAMA MUSCLE

It could be lights out for college theatre professor Nicky Abbondanza. With dead bodybuilders popping up on campus, Nicky, and his favorite colleague/life partner Noah Oliver, must use their drama skills to figure out who is taking down pumped up musclemen in the Physical Education building before it is curtain down for Nicky and Noah. Complicating matters is a visit from Noah's parents from Wisconsin, and Nicky's suspicion that Noah may be hiding more than a cut, smooth body. You will be applauding and shouting Bravo for Joe Cosentino's fast-paced, side-splittingly funny, edge-of-your-seat entertaining second novel in this delightful series. Curtain up and weights up!

2015-2016 Rainbow Award Honorable Mention

DRAMA CRUISE

Theatre professors and couple, Nicky Abbondanza and Noah Oliver, are going overboard as usual, but this time on an Alaskan cruise, where dead college theatre professors are popping up everywhere from the swimming pool to the captain's table. Further complicating matters are Nicky's and Noah's parents as surprise cruise passengers, and Nicky's assignment to direct a murder mystery dinner theatre show onboard ship. Nicky and Noah will need to use their drama skills to figure out who is bringing the curtain down on vacationing theatre professors before it is lights out for the handsome couple. You will be applauding and shouting Bravo for Joe Cosentino's fast-paced, side-splittingly funny, edge-of-your-seat entertaining third novel in this delightful series. Curtain up and ship ahoy!

DRAMA DETECTIVE

Theatre professor Nicky Abbondanza is directing *Sherlock Holmes, the Musical* in a professional summer stock production at Treemeadow College, co-starring his husband and theatre professor colleague, Noah Oliver, as Dr. John Watson. When cast members begin toppling over like hammy actors at a curtain call, Nicky dons Holmes' persona onstage and off. Once again Nicky and Noah will need to use their drama skills to figure out who is lowering the street lamps on the actors before the handsome couple get half-baked on Baker Street. You will be applauding and shouting Bravo for Joe Cosentino's fast-paced, side-splittingly funny, edge-of-your-seat entertaining fifth novel in this delightful series. Curtain up, the game is afoot!

DRAMA FRATERNITY

Theatre professor Nicky Abbondanza is directing *Tight End Scream Queen*, a slasher movie filmed at Treemeadow College's football fraternity house, co-starring his husband and theatre professor colleague, Noah Oliver. When young hunky cast members begin fading out with their scenes, Nicky and Noah will once again need to use their drama skills to figure out who is sending the quarterback, jammer, wide receiver, and more to the cutting room floor before Nicky and Noah hit the final reel. You will be applauding and shouting Bravo for Joe Cosentino's fast-paced, side-splittingly funny, edge-of-your-seat entertaining sixth novel in this delightful series. Lights, camera, action, frat house murders!

DRAMA CASTLE

Theatre professor Nicky Abbondanza is directing a historical film at a castle in Scotland, co-starring his spouse, theatre professor Noah Oliver, and their son Taavi. When historical accuracy disappears along with hunky men in kilts, Nicky and Noah will once again need to use their drama skills to figure out who is pitching residents of Conall Castle off the drawbridge and into the moat, before Nicky and Noah land in the dungeon. You will be applauding and shouting Bravo for Joe Cosentino's fast-paced, side-splittingly funny, edge-of-your-seat entertaining seventh novel in this delightful series. Take your seats. The curtain is going up on steep cliffs, ancient turrets, stormy seas, misty moors, malfunctioning kilts, and murder!

Drama Dance

Theatre professor Nicky Abbondanza is back at Treemeadow College directing their Nutcracker Ballet co-starring his spouse, theatre professor Noah Oliver, their son Taavi, and their best friend and department head, Martin Anderson. With muscular dance students and faculty in the cast, the Christmas tree on stage isn't the only thing rising. When cast members drop faster than their loaded dance belts, Nicky and Noah will once again need to use their drama skills to figure out who is cracking the Nutcracker's nuts, trapping the Mouse King, and being cavalier with the Cavalier, before Nicky and Noah end up stuck in the Land of the Sweets. You will be applauding and shouting Bravo for Joe Cosentino's fast-paced, side-splittingly funny, edge-of-your-seat entertaining eighth novel in this delightful series. Take your seats. The curtain is going up on the Fairy — Sugar Plum that is, clumsy mice, malfunctioning toys, and murder!

Drama Faerie

It's summer at Treemeadow College's new Globe Theatre, where theatre professor Nicky Abbondanza is directing a musical production of *A Midsummer Night's Dream* co-starring his spouse, theatre professor Noah Oliver, their son Taavi, and their best friend and department head, Martin Anderson. With an all-male, skimpily dressed cast and a love potion gone wild, romance is in the starry night air. When hunky students and faculty in the production drop faster than their tunics and tights, Nicky and Noah will need to use their drama skills to figure out who is taking swordplay to the extreme before Nicky and Noah end up foiled in the forest. You will be applauding and shouting Bravo for Joe Cosentino's fast-paced, side-splittingly funny, edge-of-your-seat entertaining ninth novel in this delightful series. Take your seats. The curtain is going up on star-crossed young lovers, a faerie queen, an ass who is a great Bottom, and murder!

Drama Runway

It's spring break at Treemeadow College, and theatre professor Nicky Abbondanza is directing a runway show for the Fashion Department. Joining him are his spouse, theatre professor Noah Oliver, their son Taavi, and their best friend and department head, Martin Anderson. Designed by visiting professor Ulla Ultimate, the show is bound to be the ultimate event of the season. And bound it is with designs featuring black leather and chains. When sexy male models drop faster than their leather chaps, Nicky and Noah will need to use their drama skills to figure out who is taking the term "a cut male model" literally before Nicky and Noah end up steamed in the wardrobe steamer. You will be applauding and shouting Bravo for Joe Cosentino's fast-paced, side-splittingly funny, edge-of-your-seat entertaining tenth novel in this delightful series. Take your seats. The runway is lighting up with hunky models, volatile designers, bitter exes, newfound lovers, and murder!

Drama Christmas *(coming soon)*

It's winter holiday time at Treemeadow College, and Theatre Professor Nicky Abbondanza, his husband Theatre Associate Professor Noah Oliver, their son Taavi, and best friends Martin and Ruben are donning their gay apparel in a musical version of Scrooge's *A Christmas Carol*, entitled *Call Me Carol!* More than stockings are hung when hunky chorus members drop like snowflakes. Once again, our favorite thespians will need to use their drama skills to catch the killer and make the yuletide gay before their Christmas balls get cracked. You will be applauding and shouting Bravo for Joe Cosentino's fast-paced, side-splittingly funny, edge-of-your-seat entertaining eleventh novel in this delightful series. Take your seats. The stage lights are coming up on an infamous miser, S&M savvy ghost, Victorian lovers of the past, present, and future, a not so Tiny Tim, and murder!

Books by Joe Cosentino

Made in the USA
Las Vegas, NV
28 July 2021